Formatting by Dawn Nelson
Cover design by Dawn Nelson

For Donna, as a thank you for helping to
make this book the best it can be.
Your help has been invaluable.
xxx

# Loch Ness

D A NELSON

# DANELSON

# Chapter 1

## Summer, 1893

Caledonian Central Station was busy. Humans and creatures hurried from train to platform to exit in a constant flow of bodies. The place was awash with the hissing and chugging of the green liveried steam engines as they entered and departed Glasgow's finest departure point. There was a heavy stench of burning coal mixed with the sweet scent of water vapour and the air was alive with the sounds of city life: footsteps too numerous to count, whistles being blown, guards shouting, people chatting and the colourful stall holders yelling their wares. As a country girl, I revelled in this new found excitement and couldn't help but stare at the office girls as they walked by in their pretty patterned dresses and beautifully decorated straw hats.

I was to meet him under the big clock in the centre of the station at noon. I was to wait there to be given further instructions. My stomach churned at the thought of what lay ahead. Here was me , Esther Abercrombie, a recent graduate of the Ellen Campbell Secretarial School, waiting to start my new life with a man who was world famous. Dr . Thaddeus Dwell was a celebrated cryptozoologist, explorer and inventor who had chosen me from an unknown number of applicants to be his secretary. I hadn't yet met him. My interview had taken place over a series of letters, and I was excited and trepidatious about meeting him. All I knew was that he was coming from London to the north to start a new study and I was to join him.

So, there I was, standing there alone, waiting for a stranger to take me on a big adventure. Some he-elves in multi-coloured suits walked by, one tipped his bowler hat at me and I blushed. I was not used to getting any attention, my mother forbade it. 'Esther ,' she would say, 'that's the devil's work and, anyway, you're far too plain to attract any man.' A human man bustled past me, catching my skirts and the carpet bag at my feet with his black umbrella. He apologised, tipped his hat and rushed over towards the ticket collector. A flower seller, a fairy in purple skirt and starched blouse, offered me a bunch of bright blue delphiniums, but I shook my head. Her smile faded immediately, and she turned away, wings drooping in disappointment.

I looked around me once more, fearing Dr . Dwell was not coming after all, and he had asked me to stand there as some sort of cruel joke. A tug on the back of my skirts was the first I became aware someone was trying to get my attention. I immediately turned around and then looked down. Standing before me was a gorgeously attired dwarf who introduced himself as Cassius Ironblood of the Underlands. He was dressed in a brilliant red velvet jacket, colourful silk waistcoat, and black trousers. His long silver hair was tied back in a ribbon and his beard had been fashioned into a neat plait.

'Miss Abercrombie, I presume?' the dwarf said. He gave me a small bow. 'Cassius Ironblood.'

'I am.' I curtsied. 'Pleased to meet you, Mr. Ironblood.'

'I am Dr . Dwell's valet and righthand man,' he continued.

'He asks that you accompany me to the carriage outside, where he awaits you.'

I was somewhat taken aback by this introduction. Surely Dr. Dwell had said in his letter he would meet me himself? It was what I expected, but I said nothing. Dr . Dwell was a great man and, of course, he would send a servant to meet me. What was I thinking? Cassius turned about and walked towards the exit and the taxi rank outside. Without hesitation, I picked up my carpet bag, adjusted my shawl and followed. A porter, in a dark blue suit, scuttled after me, pushing a cart holding my travel trunk. It was small compared to others I had seen go through the station and held all my worldly goods.

A gorgeous cavalcade of five shiny black steam carriages was waiting for me when I exited the sandstore palace that was the station. Driven by metal man-shaped automatons in tall black hats, the carriages were decorated with scrolls and swirls of gold, and the golden livery mark of TD. The door of the first carriage opened and a tall, older man wearing a travelling cloak and carrying a silver topped cane climbed down. He smiled displaying an array of perfectly white teeth and walked towards me with his gloved hand outstretched.

'Miss Abercrombie, so glad to make your acquaintance,' he said. I caught a whiff of expensive cologne. His eyes were shining with enthusiasm. 'My name is Thaddeus Dwell, and I am delighted that you decided to join us.'

'Very pleased to meet you Dr . Dwell,' I said shyly, shaking his hand. Like the dwarf, Dr . Dwell was expensively and beautifully dressed. Under the cloak, he wore a grey morning suit, red silk waistcoat, matching cravat and a shiny black top hat which he doffed politely. He replaced the hat, then offered me his arm.

'May I escort you into the carriage?' he said, a smile playing about his lips. 'Then you can tell me all about yourself.' As I took his arm, Dwell nodded to Cassius, who took my bag and carefully stowed it in one of the other carriages with my travel trunk. Then I found myself guided towards the front car where Dwell stopped to help me inside.

I had never ridden in a steam carriage before and was almost disappointed to discover that, apart from the small steam engine and the automaton at the front, there was little difference to a horse-drawn one. The carriage itself was comfortable with its horsehair stuffed velvet benches, and Dr . Dwell made sure I was settled before taking the seat opposite. He rapped on the top of the carriage with his cane. There came a short bell ring in reply, and then the carriage hissed and steamed. There was a creaking and a groaning before a violent judder that made me nearly fall out of my seat.

'Oops,' Dwell said apologetically, 'I need to work on that!'

Then, with a groan, the carriage moved forward and left the rank. I looked out of the curtained window as the station moved out of view.

'I'm very pleased you decided to join me on this expedition, Miss Abercrombie,' Dwell said. 'Have I said that already? I think I might have.' He was a handsome man of his middle years with greying hair and dark mutton chops. His blue eyes twinkled, and I was immediately put at ease.

'I'm delighted to be here, Dr . Dwell,' I replied. 'It's the first time I've been so far away from home.'

'Well, I can tell you we are going to have such an adventure!' he replied, clapping his hands.

'Where exactly are we going, Dr. Dwell? You didn't say in your last letter.' I was somewhat nervous about going anywhere with a man I did not know, and my mother was horrified at the impropriety of it. It took a letter from Dwell reassuring her his intentions towards me were pure plus a sweetener of two pounds to finally put her mind at rest.

'We're going on a hunt for an elusive creature,' he said, eyes brilliant, 'and you, my dear, will bear witness to my study of it. I want you to take notes during the day and act as a typist for me when I come to write about this expedition.'

'What creature?' I asked, thinking of all the creatures that already inhabited our world. Apart from the fae, there were dwarves, satyrs, centaurs, and fauns. Others existed, but were secretive and hard to find. Knowing what little I knew of humanity at the time, I couldn't blame them. I had witnessed children being used to clean chimneys and horses worked to death. It was no wonder they hid.

He tapped his nose. 'All in good time,' he said with a smile.

Proclaimed as the next new thing in travel, the steam carriages were certainly faster than horses, but it still took us six full hours to reach our destination. They had been invented by a man in Manchester, who was so horrified by the amount of manure produced by the city's horses; he came up with his own solution. They were expensive and rare, and it was exciting to be riding in one.

The journey wasn't terrible, but it was such a long time to be stuck inside with a stranger. I spent a good bit of it looking out of the window, watching as we left the black, soot covered streets of the elegantly built Glasgow and travelled west out into the countryside. The roads were poorer there and caused the carriage to lurch and roll, but modern technology is a wonder and we did not get stuck in the numerous potholes along the way. We turned north at Dumbarton, then headed along the twisting narrow Loch Lomond road that served as the only entranceway to the Highlands.

'Where are we heading to, Dr . Dwell?' I asked, staring out at the calm stretch of deep blue water framed either side by the reaching purple mountains and green hills of the lower Highlands.

'Alright, I'll tell you,' he replied, 'but you must keep it a secret until we arrive. Do you promise?'

I nodded.

'Strone,' he said and gave me such a look of triumph that I felt stupid for not knowing why we would go there. I must have given him a quizzical look, for he laughed. 'It's a small hamlet on Loch Ness near Urquhart Castle. Don't worry, my dear, we have a good reason and I'll tell you over dinner tonight at the inn.'

I did venture to ask why we had not taken the railway to Inverness and then by carriage to the nearby Drumnadrochit. The new stretch of the line between Aviemore and Inverness had opened the previous year, making the area far more accessible. Dwell just gave me a withering look and refused to answer, so I went back to my window, watching and day dreaming.

It was dark and raining when we arrived at Strone. Not the kind of rain to soak through a woollen cloak, but a light smirr. I had been sleeping for the latter part of the journey and, as I got down from the carriage, the light spray on my face was enough to wake me to full alertness. I looked around me. We had stopped outside a large whitewashed house with a small stone porch and a painted wooden sign declaring it to be the Strone Inn. Lanterns lit up the downstairs windows, giving it a cosy air, and there were sounds of men talking from the bar inside. Dwell, who had been directing the unpacking of the carriages by the automatons, turned to Cassius.

'Take Miss Abercrombie inside and see she is settled,' he said. Cassius bowed and accompanied me inside.

The inn was basic, but clean. We were met at the door by our smiling hostess, who introduced herself as Mrs. Mackintosh. She was a small woman of about 50 years with white hair that had been scraped back into a tight bun. Her face was youthful, and she had the light step of a woman half her age. She beckoned us in and had her son, Adam, a sullen lad of around 15, show us up to our rooms. The stairwell was dark and creaking, Adam's candle throwing up ghoulish shadows on the walls, but having grown up in a small farmhouse in the country, the dark did not scare me. I followed him to the first floor, where he took me along to the end of the corridor.

My room was at the front of the inn and had a view of the famous Loch Ness, or so the morose youth reluctantly told me. He parroted a whole diatribe of facts and information about the surrounding area, words that I was sure his mother had forced him to repeat for every visitor. Adam lit the oil lamp sitting on a small vanity table and moved to the door.

'Is that all you need, missus?' he asked. I nodded. 'Then mum said you've to come down to the inn to get yer tea.'

'Thank you.'

As the youth left, I removed my shawl and placed my reticule on the bed. The room was sparingly furnished, but was comfortable enough. There was a large bed against one wall next to a small fireplace that was unlit. A chest of drawers stood opposite and the pristine white-washed walls were decorated with framed, dried flowers. A fraying rug covered the floor, deadening the sounds of my footsteps on the wooden floor as I explored the room. I turned back to the bed and was delighted to find the bedding fresh and pristine. I smiled. This will do well, I thought.

It was a far cry from the bedroom I shared with my three sisters. I couldn't believe it: I was getting to sleep in my own room, in my own bed. What luck!

There was a knock at the door.

'Come in!'

Dr . Dwell stuck his head in.

'I heard Mrs. Mackintosh has laid on some supper for us,' he said, eyes sparkling in the dull lamplight. 'Shall we go down together?'

I grabbed my bag and joined him in the corridor, carefully closing my bedroom door behind me. He offered me his arm and together; we went down to dine.

The public bar was lively. A large room with a sooty fireplace at one end, it was packed with chattering local men enjoying an evening pint. We could hear their chatter and laughter as we approached the entrance. As we walked into the room, the babble suddenly stopped and all eyes were on us. Dwell paused. His eyes darted around, taking in the various dress of the Highlanders. They were outfitted in similar suits of tweed in muted brown tones and all to a man donned a flat cap and a curious gaze.

'Good evening gentlemen,' Dwell said as he ushered me forward. He led me to the bar where Mrs. Mackintosh was holding court. She poured bottled beer into a pewter mug and gave it to a customer who was standing nearby.

'Dr . Dwell, Miss Abercrombie,' she said, beaming. 'I've put you in the snug over there,' she added with a nod in the direction of the fire. 'Adam will be out shortly with your supper.'

'Thank you, Mrs. Mackintosh,' Dwell replied. 'Now, before I accompany my charming companion to dinner, could I order some wine for us? The best you have.'

'Of course,' she said, eyes bright in lantern light. 'You get yourselves settled and I'll bring it over.'

Supper was a plate of fresh grilled trout with buttered bread, carrots, and potatoes. Although simple, it was welcome fare, and I tucked in greedily. I washed the whole lot down with a glass of fruity red wine brought to us by our lady inn owner. Unused to alcohol, the wine went straight to my head and, in the warmth of the inn, by the flickering light of the log fire, I began to relax.

'What a marvellous start to our adventure,' Dwell said, wiping his mouth with a red silk handkerchief produced from his own pocket. 'There's nothing quite so tasty as fresh trout in a Highland inn .'

'It was delicious,' I replied. I paused to stare into the flames of the fire. They danced merrily, sometimes hissing as rain water slid down the chimney to meet its fiery death. 'What are we doing here, Dr . Dwell?' I said at last. 'You haven't yet told me.'

'Well,' he began. Then he looked around him and pulled his chair closer to the bench on which I sat. He leaned in and said in a low voice: 'I was going to wait until tomorrow to tell you, but there's no reason why I should n't tell you now . We're here to study the monster.'

'Monster? The Loch Ness monster?' I said aloud. He gave me a look and put his finger to his lips. Then he poured me another glass of wine from the bottle left by our hostess. I took a sip.

'The very same,' he said in hushed tones.

'But it's just a myth,' I replied, 'a folk tale.'

'Is it?' He looked at me like I was the mad one, then leaned back and smiled. 'Miss Abercrombie, your face is a picture.'

'So, we're not here for the monster?' My head was befuddled with wine and I couldn't make out whether he was joking or not.

'Oh, no, we are,' he said. 'I'm here to study it and you are here to help me.'

His intention, he then told me, was to do a detailed study of the creature in its habitat and then publish a memoir about his adventures. My role was to take notes. There would also be a speaking tour.

'Of course, the newspapers are going to love this!' he added, looking particularly pleased with himself. 'This latest discovery will put me on the map as the greatest cryptozoologist in all of the British Empire… no, the world.' He fanned his hands in a semi-circle as he said this and looked off into the distance. I don't know what he expected from me, but after a few moments, he put his hands down and frowned. 'You don't seem excited,' he said.

'I am very excited,' I told him, although this was not true. I knew Dr. Dwell was a well-known cryptozoologist. Indeed, he had made many important discoveries of magical creatures over the past few years. However, I was not sure that this was a quest he would be successful in. 'I'm just a little tired after the long journey. I think I will retire now.' I stood up. 'I promise you I will be more lively tomorrow.'

'Such a good idea, my dear,' he replied. 'Of course, you are exhausted.'

He stood politely.

'Goodnight Dr. Dwell,' I said.

'Goodnight, Miss Abercrombie. I shall see you down here by eight o'clock sharp for breakfast.'

I nodded and took my leave, pausing momentarily at the door to look back. Dwell had sat down again and was supping on his wine. He did not see me looking. As I turned, I nearly tripped over Cassius, who had scuttled into the inn sopping wet.

'Oh, sir,' I said. 'You must dry yourself at the fire before you catch your death of cold.'

The dwarf looked up at me with sad eyes and nodded. Saying nothing, he walked past me and made his way to his master. I turned and walked out.

In the hallway, I paused again. My head was addled. I could not think straight and cursed myself for consuming two glasses of wine. The door was only just there, so I opened it and walked out to get some fresh air for a moment. Sheltered from the rain in the little stone porch, I closed my eyes and took in a deep breath. The air was clean and sweet, so unlike the smog-ridden atmosphere of Glasgow earlier that day. As I opened them, I became aware I was not alone. Twenty yards away, silhouetted against the soft light of a window, stood the most magnificent black horse I had ever seen. It was around 18 hands high, about the height of a Clydesdale, and had a shiny jet coat. The horse did not have a saddle, but sported a silver bridle that jingled gently as it moved. We stood staring at each other for a few moments. I felt that it was weighing me up, trying to decide whether I was dangerous or not. Then, as soon as it had appeared, it was away again. It turned and moved off, its huge feet barely making a sound on the dirt road, and disappeared into depths of the night. I stood there for a few minutes more, wondering. Then I began to shiver. Re-entering the house, I shut the door and climbed the stairs to bed. Exhausted, weary, dead on my feet; I was all of those. I just wanted to close my eyes and think of nothing more until the morning. But that horse had somehow entered my mind and stayed there, and it was several hours before I could sleep

# Chapter 2

The next morning, a loud thumping on my bedroom door woke me. I got out of bed and gingerly put my warm feet on the freezing floorboards. The fire had not yet been lit and even though it was summer, there was a chill in the air. Wrapping a shawl around myself, I staggered to the door and opened it a crack. I looked out, but there was no-one there. I heard a gentle cough. Looking down, I found myself gazing into the large brown eyes of Cassius Ironblood.

'The master asks if you would join him for breakfast,' he said, face flushed. Was he embarrassed at waking me?

'Could you tell Dr . Dwell, I will join him in around half an hour?' I said as politely as I could. 'Thank you, Cassius.'

'Ma'am.'

I shut the door and got to work on dressing. Mrs. Mackintosh had left a pitcher of water and a clean towel in my room the evening before and I quickly washed in the ice-cold water. Then I struggled into my corset and dress. As a working-class woman, I had never had a maid to help me into my garments, but one of my sisters was usually around to help. Today, I was on my own and it took me some time and a fair bit of wriggling to tie the corset properly. Then I pulled my dress over my head. I had chosen a simple floral pattern, which I would match with a straw boater decorated with silk flowers before I went out. Quickly pinning my long dark hair up into fashionable tight curls on the top of my head, and checked myself in the mirror. My cheeks were flushed from the effort, but I looked neat and tidy. I glanced at my pocket watch. Half an hour had gone by. I should hurry. It wouldn't do to be late on my first day. As I rushed around, it suddenly dawned on me that the room was not as bright as it should be on a summer's morning. I opened the curtains and looked out. Being positioned at the front of the inn, the room had a view of the loch and it was breath-taking this morning. The sun was just rising over the mountains, highlighting the soft mist that hung like a roll of fleece on their jagged tops. Somewhere an eagle cried. I looked for it, but could not see it at first, then suddenly it was there, silhouetted in the sun, gliding low across the water. I followed its flight and watched it head north. It was a magnificent sight.

Smiling to myself, I was about to remove myself from the window when something caught my eye. In front of the inn stood a fine-looking young man in a tweed suit; a working man's outfit. He was looking up at the building with curiosity. Hatless, his jet-black hair gleamed in the sunlight, giving him an aura of something otherworldly. It had not been tamed into submission, as was the fashion of the day, but was wild and unruly. As I watched, his gaze rested on me and his demeanour changed. Giving me a cheeky wink, he performed an elegantly orchestrated bow, his long arms sweeping before him, almost touching the stony ground. He rose slowly and grinned. Alarmed by this sudden turn of events, I pulled back from the window, ashamed I had been caught snooping on him. Face burning with embarrassment, I could hear my mother's voice ringing in my ears: You know what happened to the nosey cat? Curiosity got her! It was brazen to stare at a man, let alone have him catch you watching. She had drummed that into us girls from an early age. However, there had been something about him, something untamed and fascinating, and I could not help but look out again. The forecourt in front of the inn was empty save for a couple of blackbirds. He was gone. How curious.

I mused about who the strange man had been when I went down to breakfast and promised myself, I would find out.

Thaddeus Dwell was sitting at last night's table eating a hearty breakfast of black pudding, bacon and eggs. A large teapot sat in front of him, along with a jug of milk and a plate of toast dripping with fresh butter. He rose as I approached and ushered me into a chair beside him.

'Good morning, good morning,' he said jovially as he sat down again. 'Now what can I get you for breakfast, Miss Abercrombie?'

'A cup of tea will suffice,' I said. I felt shy even though I had now known the eminent doctor for 24 hours, give or take. I still couldn't believe my luck. Here was I sitting next to such a famous man and he had hired me to help him on his latest quest.

'Miss Abercrombie, can I advise you to eat something this morning?' he said. 'It's an early start and we're going to be out all day. Mrs. Mackintosh has prepared us a picnic lunch, but we'll not be having that until much later. Why don't you ask her to prepare you a fried breakfast? It's very good.'

To emphasise his point, he forked a piece of perfectly browned bacon and popped it into his mouth. He smiled as he chewed, his eyes sparkling in delight at such delicious fare.

'No thank you,' I replied. 'I'll just have some tea. I don't usually eat this early.'

'Suit yourself.'

As I poured myself a cup, Dwell went through our agenda for the day. We were to meet a man by the name of Buchan down at the dock and he would take us out on to the loch in his boat. Cassius was to remain on land to unpack the equipment boxes and set up what Dwell termed his laboratory in the barn adjoining the inn.

'Mrs. Mackintosh has very kindly given me permission to use her barn. I've already been to see it. It's perfect for what we want it for,' he finished. He wiped his mouth with a cotton napkin and scooped up his teacup. 'This is so thrilling. I've never been on a hunt for such an elusive creature before. This will be the find of the century.'

'It certainly will, Dr . Dwell,' I replied, trying to match his enthusiasm. I still wasn't convinced the monster was real.

He held his cup up as if raising a toast. I raised mine too. 'To us, Miss Abercrombie,' he said, 'and may we be successful in our ventures.' He took a sip of his tea and I did, too.

'Now,' he said, getting serious again, 'can I ask: did you pack a good sturdy pair of Wellington boots, and your tweeds ? Mrs. Mackintosh reckons it'll rain this afternoon, and I'd hate for you to get wet and cold.'

I did not possess the boots, and I told him so, but I did have a long tweed  cloak that had served me well these past four winters.

'I'll ask Cassius to find you a pair of boots,' he replied. He stood up and looked at me. 'Have you finished your tea? No? Well, get a move on girl, we have work to do.'

My mother would have been aghast at how quickly I threw back the last remnants of my drink. I placed the cup down and hurried after Dwell, who was already striding towards the door.

'Meet me outside in ten minutes,' he said, 'and don't be late.'

I hurried upstairs, grabbed my things from my room, and was back down at the front door before the allotted time had passed. Panting a little, I fixed my straw bonnet to my head with a hatpin, threw the cloak over my shoulders and checked myself in the hall mirror. My face was a little flushed, unladylike in my mother's eyes, but other than that, I looked presentable.

'Right, I'd best be off,' I said to myself as I went to the front door. Then I paused. In the corner nearest the entrance was an elephant foot stuffed with umbrellas. Mrs. Mackintosh wouldn't mind me borrowing one of them, would she? I didn't think so. I picked up a large black umbrella, opened the door and went out to start my new job.

Dwell was waiting for me at the small wooden dock about two hundred yards from the inn's front door. He was standing directing a harassed-looking Cassius who was busy loading equipment on to a puffer boat, The Salty Barnacle. It was a stumpy little steamboat made of riveted iron with a single mast and crewed by a weather battered captain and two men. They had been busy getting it ready to depart, but, as one, stopped what they were doing to stare at me. I approached nervously.

'Miss Abercrombie,' Dwell said offering me his arm, 'may I help you on board?'

As I carefully walked up a small gangplank, the captain, who had been standing next to the entrance of the crew's quarters, rushed forward. He was a small man with a greying beard, a ruddy complexion and dark, piercing eyes.

'Jist a minute, Mr. Dwell,' he said, hand outstretched. 'You never said nothing about bringing a lassie on board.'

'And you said nothing about not bringing a lassie on board,

Captain Buchan,' said Dwell, helping me over the boat's side.

'I cannae be having a lassie on board,' the captain replied. He frowned. 'It's no right. It's bad luck.'

'Nonsense, Captain Buchan, utter nonsense,' Dwell replied. His voice was calm, but anger glittered in his eyes.

'No, I must insist,' the other man said. He was now standing beside us and he drew himself up to his full height and crossed his arms. Although human, he looked to me like an overgrown dwarf and I had to stifle a chuckle.

'I need Miss Abercrombie on board. She is my assistant,' Dwell said through gritted teeth.

'And I'm telling you it's bad luck!' retorted the captain.

Dwell breathed in deeply and changed tack.

'What would it take for you to allow Miss Abercrombie on board?' he said, looking at me. I shifted awkwardly on my feet. I did not like being the centre of an argument. The captain's eyes narrowed.

'What do you mean?'

'Would an extra three pounds help my cause?'

'Make it five – for insurance, you understand - and you have a deal.' Buchan stuck out his hand. Dwell looked at it, thought for a moment, and then shook it. The captain gave him a smile and stood back to allow me access to his craft. The rest of the crew went back to work in silence.

It took them a further ten minutes to load all of Dwell's equipment, which consisted of several wooden boxes containing electrical equipment of the explorer's own invention and a large camera. Then at last, the captain instructed the engineer to start the engine and The Salty Barnacle burst into life, puffed, shuddered and died.

'Blair, whit's going on?' Buchan shouted from the wheelhouse. There was no reply from down below, but then the engine started again and this time the little boat began to puff some more. It reversed away from the dock and took a slow turn to begin its journey along the loch. Puff, puff, puff, it went as it gently made its way out of the little harbour at Strone, heading south-east.

I positioned myself next to Dwell forward, so that we might have the best view.

Although bright, the sun had not yet burned off the dampness in the air and I was glad of my cloak as the little boat meandered up the loch. Dwell had instructed Buchan to go into the centre of the loch so that he might lower a piece of machinery he called his Octophone Listener into the water. It was, he told me, a highly sensitive listening device that could pick up the smallest sound in the water. A second device, his Camera Nerou was a waterproof camera that took images every five minutes and was also secured to the side of the boat and lowered into the mysterious water. For my part, I was to position myself next to Dwell and record everything he told me to in a leather-bound notebook. I took up position seated on a box at the front of a puffer, pencil poised over the smooth silky pages, waiting to take down Dwell's every thought.

'What do you think of this then, Miss Abercrombie?' Dwell asked as he checked the Octophone was tied securely enough to the side of the wooden boat. 'Exciting, isn't it?'

'Very much so, Dr . Dwell,' I agreed, but in truth, I was starting to feel decidedly uncomfortable. We had been travelling for some fifteen minutes now and I was feeling increasingly uneasy. It wasn't the cool air rippling over my face that was the culprit, but the creeping feeling that we were being watched. I searched the loch for signs of another boat, but we were the only craft on the water. I examined the banks of the loch, looking for any evidence of spies, but could see no one, only the dark trees and summer grasses of the shoreline. So, I kept my discomfort to myself for fear that Dwell should think I was a silly woman and waited silently for his instructions. I looked at him expectantly.

Dwell was fumbling in his jacket pocket for something and pulled out a packet of matches. He carefully lit one and used it to light his pipe. Taking a couple of puffs, he moved as far forward as he could go to the front of the bow and positioned himself there, one foot on the wooden banister.

'Take this down,' Dwell said, looking for all the world like some famous explorer. 'The thirteenth of June, 1893, here present Dr . Thaddeus Dwell, cryptozoologist and explorer, and Miss Esther Abercrombie, secretary, taking notes. Today we start our hunt for the elusive Loch Ness Monster…am I talking too fast for you Miss Abercrombie?'

I looked up from my scribbling. 'No, sir.'

'Good, good… today we start our hunt for the elusive Loch Ness Monster, a creature so shy and rare that people question whether she is real or not. With this expedition, I intend to prove one way or the other whether this creature or creatures… there may be a group of them, as you know, Miss Abercrombie… and, if they exist, to study them.' He took a puff of his pipe. 'My methods are thus: to study the loch using my own senses and an array of instruments of my own invention, including my trademarked Octophone Listener and Camera Nerou.' He paused, allowing me to catch up, then resumed again. 'Also assisting me is my long-time friend and assistant, the dwarf Cassius Ironblood, whose role is to ensure all equipment was maintained in tiptop condition, ready for use and to take photographs as a record.' Here he stopped. I waited for him to begin again. He stood puffing on his pipe for some moments, lost in thought, before turning back to me and saying: 'I think that should do for the first entry, don't you?'

'Yes, Dr . Dwell,' I replied.

'Good, good,' he said. 'You know, I've got an excellent reputation for tracking down elusive creatures. I was the first man to prove the existence of the Yeti.' He looked at me for approval and I nodded, hoping that was enough. 'And I once found a tribe of long forgotten pigmy humans. I was the first normal sized human they had ever seen, and they welcomed me like a god.' He took a puff of his pipe. 'Yes, those were good days.' He stared out over the water. 'Of course, there were only two creatures who ever eluded me.'

'There were? What were they?'

'One was the Sabre-fanged Anaconda of the Atlantic Ocean. Horrible creature it is. It normally lives far out into the ocean, but occasionally will swim inshore and snatch unsuspecting people from the shoreline.'

'And the other?'

'The Loch Ness Monster, of course. She is my dream catch.'

'Catch? You mean to catch her?'

'Just to study and put back.' He took his pipe out of his mouth and turned to face me. 'Why don't you put your pencil down for a little while and enjoy the scenery? This loch is truly beautiful. I always love being here.' He gazed off into the distance.

'You've been before?' I asked.

He started. 'What? Er… yes, a long time ago,' he said.

'Were you on holiday?' I asked.

He stared at me like he did not understand the question before pulling himself together. 'Would you like a look through my spyglass?' he asked. 'It's quite a splendid one!' Without waiting for an answer, he walked over to a beautiful rosewood box lying next to me and opened it. Inside was a brass telescope. He took it out, checked that it was working, and then handed it to me.

'Have a look through that and tell me what you can see,' he said.

Carefully, I put the spyglass to my left eye, screwing closed my right so that I might better see. The sight was blurry at first, so I made some adjustments. Training the telescope on the loch, I swung it around until I could see the banks of the loch some distance away. They were steep and covered in trees and totally clear, except for a few birds and some red squirrels. As I trained the scope around, I spotted a huge black horse standing quite still on the shoreline. It was quietly watching us and as I looked, it seemed to look straight at me through the glass.

'Oh!' I said, lowering the instrument.

'What is it?'

I looked through the glass again, and it was gone. 'I thought I saw something, a horse,' I said.

'A horse? Give me that.' He snatched the spyglass from my hand and held it up to his eye. Training it on the shore, he harrumphed and handed it back. 'There's nothing there. Stupid girl! You must have been mistaken.'

'Well, I…' I began.

He gave me a look that would have withered a lesser person, so I stopped speaking. Then he turned and strode up the deck of the puffer, leaving me wondering what I had done wrong.

I remained mute for the rest of the journey up the loch.

The sun soon burned the mist off the mountain-tops to reveal them in their true green and purple glory. The summits reached far above my head, touching a soft blue sky, and I wondered what it would be like up there. What wonders would you see?

Now that the sun was almost fully at its highest, the chill of the morning had evaporated, replaced by a sweet-scented warmth. I removed my cloak and placed it on a box next to me, and fanned myself with my notebook. It was already a beautiful day and, forgetting Dwell's rudeness earlier, I sat there enjoying, for the first time, the sensation of being utterly alive. It is hard to describe, even now, how I felt that first morning. There was the sheer, almost spiritual delight of being in such a stunning place. Loch Ness is, without a doubt, one of the most awe-inspiring places in Scotland and, maybe even, the world. I also had a sense of freedom, of purpose. I was away from home for the first time, earning my own money, making my own decisions, and that was intoxicating. I had never felt happier.

As I mused on how wonderful my new life was turning out to be, I realised that the puffer was slowing down. In fact, it pulled in at the most northern end of the loch, and the anchor was dropped.

'Miss Abercrombie, have you gone deaf?' Dwell roared. He had been calling me and I, lost in my dreamy thoughts, had not heard him.

I scrambled to my feet. 'No, Dr. Dwell,' I returned. 'I apologise.'

'Well, get over here and start taking notes,' he snapped.

He was standing near the boat's wheelhouse, setting up his equipment. The wood and brass instruments glistened and gleamed in the sunlight as he carefully positioned them on the deck.

'Here, take this,' he said, handing me the long rubber hose of the Octophone.

'What do you want me to do with it?' I said, setting down my notebook and pencil and taking the heavy snake-like object.

'Can you slowly lower it into the water off the boat's port side?' he said. 'No, not there, on the other side, foolish girl!'

I heaved the rubber hose to the other side and carefully lowered it into the inky black depths of the loch.

'A little lower,' he called. He was not looking at me, but was staring at his instrument screen. 'Lower, lower… ah! There! That's fine.'

I secured the hose in position by fastening it with some leather straps to the handrail. Then I went back to Dwell.

'Is there anything else you want me to do, sir?' I asked, excited to be an active member of the team.

'No, that's fine. Can you note down which machines were set up and at what time?'

'Yes, sir.'

The rest of the morning was spent languidly sitting on a wooden box close to the rubber hose. Dwell did not trust the hose to stay in place, so ordered me to sit next to it watching it. Every now and again, the hose would move slightly, gently pulled by the loch's undercurrents. It was a quiet and peaceful time, and I spent it staring at the dark ripples on the water, daydreaming of this and that.

'Are you still watching that hose, Miss Abercrombie?' Dwell's voice cut through my dreams. I snapped back to the present.

'Yes, I am, sir,' I assured him. I looked at him and he seemed pleased.

'Excellent.'

'Are you getting any readings yet?' I asked. I was excited about this project and really hoped we would find something.

He frowned. 'Not really, nothing big enough to make me

think Nessie is down there,' he admitted, 'but its early days. Now, back to work.'

I turned back around to look down at the hose in the water and nearly jumped out of my skin. About three feet from the surface, I saw a man's face. He was slowly rising through the water, following the rubber hose until at last he broke the surface and looked up at me, dark brown eyes full of curiosity.

# Chapter 3

You!' I whispered.

He put his finger to his lips.

I nodded, and we stayed there for some moments, staring at each other. It was the man from earlier. Although it was hard to tell, I guessed he was about 30. He had a chiselled handsome face and around his neck, shining white against his skin, was a long silver chain. His torso was naked and the rest of him… well, I didn't dare look down any further. That would not have been ladylike. We silently gazed at each other for a moment more and then, blowing me a kiss, he slowly sank under the water, quickly disappearing from view. I waited for a few minutes to see where he surfaced, but he did not reappear. Worried that something bad had happened to him, I stood up and searched the water around the boat. There was nothing to indicate he had been there, not a ripple, just a smooth, almost glass-like surface.

'Have you lost something, lass?' Buchan boomed from the wheelhouse. He was standing watching me, a cigarette dangling from his thin lips.

'No, I just… I thought…' How do you explain to someone you just saw a naked man swim under the boat? They would have thought I was mad. 'I thought I saw something,' I said. 'In the water.'

Buchan grinned. 'Aye, ye probably did. This loch is full of fish and eels. And sometimes the light plays tricks on your eyes, making you see something that wasn't there. Women particularly seem vulnerable to that. Perhaps it was that you saw.'

'Yes, perhaps that was it,' I replied. I returned to my post and sat down again. I knew what I saw, but I wasn't about to tell him that. He probably wouldn't have believed me, anyway. I wondered if my handsome visitor had been picked up by the Octophone, but it seemed not. As I glanced at Dwell, I could see he was still patiently waiting for a reading. The mystery man had not even shown up on his machine.

'Captain Buchan!' Dwell called from the other side of the boat. 'I think we had better draw up the anchor and move to another part of the loch. I'm getting very few readings here.'

'Not a problem, Mr. Dwell,' Buchan shouted. 'Now where were you thinking you'd like to go?'

Dwell looked around him. 'There were some sightings over at the western shore a couple of years ago. Over towards Balmore. Can we go there?'

'Aye, that we can,' Buchan replied. Then he began shouting orders at his men. As the First Mate Angus went to haul up the anchor, Dwell had me pulling the rubber hose back on the boat. Soon the steam engine was fired up again, its chimney throwing up little puffs of steam into the air, and the little boat was soon puffing its way further up the loch.

As we sailed, I kept a sharp eye out for the mysterious man in the water. That was twice we had seen each other, and I wanted to know more about him. But he did not reappear.

The rest of the day went fairly well. Dwell insisted on trying out several spots in the loch, but got no readings, so by the time they finished up at around 4pm, he was in a black mood.

'Take us back to Strone, Captain!' he yelled as the last of his equipment was safely stored away.

'Aye, aye!'

'Is there anything you wish me to do, Dr . Dwell?' I asked as he came to sit beside me at the rear of the little puffer.

He took out his pipe, filled it with tobacco, and lit it with a match. 'No, nothing right now, Miss Abercrombie. It's been a disappointing day, but we will find the beast if it's the last thing I do. Then you'll have plenty to write about, I can assure you.'

We docked at Strone half an hour later and I disembarked, leaving Dwell to oversee the storing of his equipment. He had instructed me to fetch Cassius, whom, he told me, would make that happen. I tried the inn first, but was told the dwarf was to be found in the barn at the side of the property.

The storage barn was, like the houses, built of stone walls with a grey slate roof. It had large wooden doors and wooden shutters covering unglazed windows. Despite being tired from my day on the loch, I hurried there and opened one of the two doors without knocking first.

'Mr. Ironblood! Mr. Ironblood!' I shouted.

Looking around me, I gasped. Straight ahead was a large iron cage complete with wrist and neck irons that were large enough to enslave an elephant. At the side sat a long metal prod attached to a contraption that was full of buttons and wheels. I could do nothing but stare at it in horror.

'Mr. Ironblood?'

'Round here!'

I skirted around the cage and found the dwarf at a grind-stone sharpening butchers' knives. Sparks flew from the machine, metal scraped on stone, as the little man brought the knives to exquisite sharpness. He placed them on top of a large wooden table once he had finished with them. He did not look up as I approached.

'What are you doing?' I asked, unsure if I was going to like the answer. I waited silently for him to answer.

'What does it look like?'

'Why do we need knives? I thought we were only going to study the monster?'

'That's right, inside and out.'

'But Dr . Dwell said we were only going to study the creature. He never said anything about killing it.'

Cassius looked up at me, and there was amusement in his eyes. 'Are you stupid?' he asked. 'How do you think Dr . Dwell always studies his finds?'

'By…watching them in their natural habitat?'

'He does that as well, then he captures them and…' He held the knife aloft and pretended to slice along his neck, feigning slitting the throat of a creature.

I felt my stomach lurch. This was not what I had agreed to. If the monster did exist, it must be left alone to live as it had always done. Killing it felt wrong in so many ways. I felt I must protest to Dwell. Now.

'So, are you going to stand there all day or are you going to tell me why you came to find me?' Cassius demanded.

I looked at him, my mind suddenly blank. 'Yes… um… oh, yes, Dr . Dwell has asked if you could go down to the jetty and unload the boat.'

Dwell was standing at the hotel bar chatting merrily to a couple of local men when I found him. He leant against the oak bar top, hand curled around a metal tankard of ale, attention completely focussed on impressing two older farmhands standing next to him. They were standing there, mesmerised by the tale he was relating. I was sure he had seen my arrival, but he'd chosen to continue his loud account of his travels in the Himalayas during an expedition to find the Yeti. As I stood at his side waiting for him to acknowledge me, he blatantly ignored me. It wasn't until I finally got fed up and touched his arm that he deigned to finally notice me. He turned around and glared at me.

'Dr. Dwell, do you have a moment?' I asked. I did not mean to come across as timid, but manners prevented me from being more aggressive. Even in these modern times, women were still supposed to be gentle and kind.

'What is it, Miss Abercrombie?' His voice was jovial, but I could see a coldness in his eyes. I felt a shiver crawl down by back.

'I wanted to ask about the… err… equipment in the barn,' I replied. I glanced at Dwell's drinking companions and they were looking at me with curiosity.

Dwell gave me a tight smile. 'Not right now, Miss Abercrombie, I'm rather busy with these gentlemen.' He nodded towards the men and winked. The men grinned.

'But – '

'That is all, Miss Abercrombie.' His voice was calm, but there were icy undertones that told me there was no point in arguing. I recognised it immediately; my own father had often used it on me and my siblings. So, I suppressed the objection that rose to my lips, gave him a curt nod and turned tail, humiliated and upset. I was just walking towards the exit when my attention was caught by the landlady.

'Miss Abercrombie!'

Mrs. Mackintosh was standing at a door I assumed led

through to the kitchen. She was holding a tray laden with food.

'Dr . Dwell said you wished to eat your dinner in your room,' she said, walking towards me. 'Here.' She handed me the tray. 'You might as well take it up with you while you go.'

I gave her a weak smile and took the tray from her. I could feel Dwell's eyes on me and wondered why he had instructed this to happen. Alright, the day had not gone as Dwell had hoped, but why banish me to my room? Why not have dinner with me as he had had the previous evening? Was this how it was going to be? Me at the mercy of his moods? I thanked Mrs. Mackintosh and left the bar, wondering if I had made a mistake taking this job.

I ate a meal of steak pie and vegetables sitting on my bed. Mrs. Mackintosh had also supplied a small tankard of delicious beer, which I finished off with relish. It was just after 6pm when I finished and, not knowing what else to do with myself, I returned the tray to the bar. Captain Buchan and his small crew were sitting near the fire swapping stories as I entered and Dwell was sitting at a table in the corner with Cassius, deep in conversation. Neither looked up as I walked through the bar to return the tray and dishes to Mrs. Mackintosh. She looked at me quizzically as I handed it over.

'Are you quite well, Miss Abercrombie?' she asked as she accepted the tray.

I gave her a small smile. 'I am, Mrs. Mackintosh.'

'It's only that you didn't join the menfolk for something to eat,' she replied.

'Well, that was not my idea,' I replied and then immediately regretted it. My inability to keep my thoughts to myself had landed me in trouble before, and I did not want my churlish comment to get back to Dwell. He was already in a strange mood with me. I did not want to make that worse. I needed this job. 'I mean… I'm sure Dr . Dwell had his reasons…'

She looked at me and winked. 'Don't worry, lass, you're not the first woman I've seen to be treated in such a way by men.' She looked over at Dwell and Cassius, who still seemed oblivious to the fact I was there. 'They're always so wrapped up in themselves, in their own supposed greatness, that they can't see women. Not really. I had a man like that myself.'

I didn't know how to respond to that.

'My late husband, Rab.' There was a twinkle in her eye. 'Yes, he was a selfish pig who did no work. He was always in the bar talking. Talking, talking, talking. He talked so much I thought his tongue would wither away. Best thing that ever happened to me was when he died.'

I looked at her askance. 'Mrs. Mackintosh, surely you don't mean that?'

'Oh, I do. He was a lazy, good for nothing man,' she replied, 'but one good thing did come out of our union… his laziness was my salvation. While he busied himself with his cronies, I learned the business. I learned how to be independent and that is why I am in such a secure position now. I have the bar; I have my own money and I am strong enough to know I will never let a man rule over me again.' She winked. 'Mark my words, Miss Abercrombie, never rely on a man.'

With that, she took the tray and disappeared into a back room with it, leaving me to mull over what she had said. It was as I was turning away with the intention of leaving the bar that I heard my name being called.

'Miss Abercrombie!' It was Dwell. 'Why don't you come and

join us?' He was in a much better mood.

'Maybe later, Dr . Dwell,' I replied. 'I have some notes to write up.'

He seemed puzzled at my refusal, almost disappointed. 'Ah, right, of course. Well, don't let me keep you.'

I nodded and returned to my room. I had no intention of doing any further work that evening. Instead, it was my plan to take a walk along the shore. My head was still full of the mysterious man in the water, the same man I had seen from my window that morning, and I hoped that I might run into him again. He intrigued me and I wanted to ask him what he had been doing. What am I saying? That wasn't all that fascinated me about him. He was handsome, that was certain, but it wasn't just his good looks that my mind kept wandering back to. He had something about him. I couldn't put my finger on it. I fetched my shawl from the hook behind the door and left.

# Chapter 4

The evening sun was already halfway to setting when I left the inn, but there was still some heat in the air. Even so, I still placed my shawl over the crook of my arm just in case it grew colder later, and sauntered towards the small pier. There was hardly a soul around as I wandered down to the water. I looked out over the black depths and wondered at its secrets. Was there really a monster living under those inky waters? Part of me hoped there was, for to find such a creature would be astounding. However, the knowledge as to what Dwell intended to do to it made me feel sick. If the Loch Ness Monster existed, how could he even contemplate killing something so rare? It was unthinkable. And cruel. The sound of metal falling in the storage barn interrupted my thoughts. It was as if something heavy had crashed on to the ground. My first instinct was to run back into the inn to fetch Dwell and Ironblood, but something made me pause. Then that part of my personality, the rash side, the side that always landed me in trouble, took over, and I hurried towards the barn to investigate. On my own.

There were no further sounds coming from the building, but I sensed a presence inside. I snuck up to the door. The lock had been torn off, and the door was standing ajar. I peeked inside, but could see nothing. Carefully opening the wooden door, I slipped inside and had a look around. The barn was in darkness, but from the dull light streaming through the entranceway, I could make out the shape of a tall dark man standing over by the cage and knives. He was oblivious to my presence.

'What are you doing in here?' I shouted, my voice wavering slightly from nerves.

He started and looked over towards me. The light streaming through the door picked out his face and bare torso. It was the handsome man from the loch. My stomach flipped. He was here.

'What are these for?' He motioned towards the cage and other equipment. His voice had a sing-song lilt common for Highland folk.

'Those are Dr . Dwell's property,' I replied. 'You shouldn't be in here.'

'What are they for?'

'I… I'm not sure.'

'Does your master plan to capture a creature and kill it?'

I did not answer.

'For that's what it looks like,' he continued. 'Is he after the monster?'

I bit my lip.

'Answer me, girl!' he growled.

I looked away. 'Yes, I think so.'

'And you're helping him?'

'I…'

He strode towards me, as graceful as a racehorse. He was a tall, well-built man with an athletic body and he was wearing only a pair of trousers. His feet were bare and his hair was wet and uncombed. I was rooted to the spot as he came to a stop right in front of me. He glared at me.

'You're helping him, yes?'

'I'm his assistant,' I replied, unable to look into those brown eyes again. 'I take down notes and write up his findings.'

'And you are happy he is planning to kill this beautiful creature?'

I looked up then. His eyes were searching mine, looking for the truth.

'I'm sure Dr . Dwell only means to study the monster, not… kill it,' I said, but even I didn't believe what I was saying.

He grunted. 'Then what is this for?' He held up a knife. It was almost touching my nose, and I took a step back in alarm, lost my footing and fell backwards onto a pile of wooden boxes. As I went down, I heard the knife clatter on the ground and felt two strong hands grab my arms just as I was about to hit wood. I gasped as he pulled me to my feet.

'Are you alright?' He seemed concerned I could have melted into those arms.

'I- I think so.'

'You could have really hurt yourself there,' he said. He was still holding me, but loosened his grip. He was looking at me curiously. 'I'm sorry if I alarmed you.'

'It's… it's alright,' I replied, freeing myself from his grasp. 'I just didn't expect it, that's all. It's not every day a strange man pulls a knife on you.'

'I'm sorry. I sometimes forget how to be a proper…' He was about to say something, but pulled himself up short.

He studied my face. It was as if he'd never seen a woman before.

'Your eyes are blue,' he said. His face was now so close to

mine I could feel the warmth of his breath.

'Yes.'

'And what are those marks on your face?'

'Freckles.'

'Huh.'

It took all my willpower to stand still while this man inspected me. I don't know why I didn't step back. It was as if I was under a spell. I couldn't take my eyes off of him. He had clear pale skin, large eyes, a long straight nose and a strong jawline. His hair was almost black and jaw length. It was not styled in the fashion of the day; it was not styled at all. It was as if he had just run his fingers through it and left it as was. It looked silky and soft, and I felt the urge to touch it.

'What is your name?'

'Esther Abercrombie.' It was then I suddenly remembered my upbringing. I stuck out my hand. 'And you are?'

He looked down at my hand, frowned, and looked back at me again. His eyes were burning with such intensity, I felt myself flush. 'My name is Duncan,' he said in a low voice.

Just then, a sound from the direction of the door broke the spell. I glanced towards it and by the time I looked back, Duncan was gone. I turned my attention back to the door where I saw Cassius Ironblood enter, carrying a wooden box laden with fish.

'Miss Abercrombie,' he said with surprise, 'what are you doing in here?'

'I-er... I had gone out for a breath of fresh air and saw that the door was open to the barn, so I thought I had better investigate,' I replied, truthfully.

'And what did you find?' He placed the heavy box on the dirt floor.

'Nothing,' I wrapped my shawl around me. 'It seems whomever broke the lock is now no longer here. Now, if you'll excuse me, I will continue on my walk.'

I sauntered past him and made for the door.

'Don't go too far,' he called after me. 'I hear there's danger in the woods around here. Strange creatures and the like.'

I turned around and feigned a casual interest. 'Oh?'

'Yes, they say the wild folk are around again.'

'The wild folk?' My thoughts immediately went to the handsome Duncan.

Cassius smirked. 'Yes, it's the locals' name for gypsies, thieves and the like. I've not seen any hide nor hair of them, but that doesn't mean they're not there. Just be careful, that's all.'

'Thank you for the warning, Mr. Ironblood, I will.'

I didn't see Duncan again for several days. And neither did we see the monster. Despite trying to entice it with fish, Dwell was not successful. It seemed that either his ploys were not working or the creature did not exist, and it put him in a foul mood. I did my job to the best of my ability, jotting down his thoughts and experiments, and kept out of his way as much as I could. I had been on the end of his cruel tongue a few times during our frequent expeditions on the loch, and I wasn't keen to take any more. As soon as the puffer docked, I disembarked and retired to my room to finish my notes and avoid the doctor at all costs. It seemed to please him that I excused myself in this way, for nothing I did was ever good enough for him and he even went as far as to blame me for the missing beast.

Things came to a head on the fourth day.

I breakfasted in my room as usual and, after dropping the tray back with Mrs. Mackintosh, I strolled down the dock only to see the boat pushing off without me. I ran down to the pier and called out to Dwell, who was seated at the stern. He looked back at me and smirked.

'Dr . Dwell! Dr . Dwell!' I shouted, but he turned around again and ignored me.

'He says having a woman on board was bringing him bad luck,' a voice at my side said. I jumped, looked down and saw Cassius standing there. 'So, he decided to go without you.'

'Well, what am I supposed to do?' I wailed. 'I'm supposed to be working.' This really wasn't on. Dwell should have told me to my face. Instead, he had snuck off without me.

Cassius shrugged. 'You may do whatever you want.'

As he walked away, I surveyed the loch. I had an unexpected free day, and I suddenly knew exactly what I wanted to do. I returned to the hotel bar and summoned Mrs. Mackenzie. She arrived from the kitchen with a dish towel slung over one shoulder and a plate of food, which she placed in front of a customer seated at the bar.

'Mrs. Mackenzie, you wouldn't happen to have a map of this area, would you?'

She looked at me and frowned. Then she bit her lip. 'I might have. I'm sure Rab had one at some point. Give me a minute.'

She lifted a hinged section of the bar top and came into the room. Motioning for me to follow, she made her way to a large dresser in the hotel's hallway. As I watched, she began to rifle through one of the drawers.

'Ah, here it is!' She handed me crumpled, folded paper. 'That's what you're looking for.'

I took the map, thanked her, and went back outside. I opened it up and studied the area. There were a few paths marked on the map that seemed interesting, but first I intended to explore Urquhart Castle. It was a short walk away and would give me a lovely view of the loch. Folding the map up, I placed it in a pocket inside my skirts and began to walk towards the loch-side.

It was a pleasant day; the sun was high in the sky and there was barely a cloud. I soon began to regret bringing my shawl. It wasn't long before I was forced to take it off and carry it. I continued walking, dressed only in my skirts, a white leg-of-mutton blouse and waistcoat. I did not want to return to the hotel, so, as I neared the ruins of Urquhart Castle, I found a dry rock on which to leave the shawl, intending to return for it on my way back.

According to a local history book I had been reading in my room, Urquhart Castle was founded in the 13th century as a stronghold of the Clan Grant. However, it had been abandoned in the middle of the 17th century and partially destroyed in 1692 to prevent it being used by Jacobite forces during the uprising. It had lain in ruins ever since, but this did not detract from the majesty and magic of the place. Sitting on a promontory on the edge of Loch Ness, it was still splendid to look at despite its decayed state and I was excited to explore it.

As I approached the dry moat, I could see that the castle was completely deserted by any living things, save for sheep and the odd bird. I scrambled down the dry moat and up the other side as quickly as I could. It was not a particularly arduous climb, but in long skirts, it was near impossible. Quickly looking around me to make sure I was not being watched, I hitched up my skirts, gathered them through my legs and tucked them in my skirt belt. I had seen it done by fisher women hunting for clams near my hometown and I knew it was an effective way to free up my legs. I scrambled up the other side, restored my skirts and my dignity and moved towards the old gatehouse.

The castle must have once been a thing to behold, but now

the curtain walls were crumbling, the roofs were off long ago, and most of the buildings were shells of their former selves. Weeds had sprung up between fallen stones and holes had been punched in walls, but despite this, the castle was still impressive.

I entered through the arched gate and paused. Looking up, I could see where once there had been a portcullis. Running my ungloved hand over the stones, feeling their cold rugged-ness, I imagined what it must have been like to have lived there hundreds of years ago. I always did this. It was my way of con-necting with the stonemasons who had built the castle and with the people who had once called it home. After a few minutes of contemplation, I continued into the main castle itself.

To my left were the remains of several buildings and an old tower. To my right, a more open space and yet more ruins of buildings. I turned left first and began to explore. The old tower caught my attention immediately, and it was to there I went first. It was largely still intact, save for a large chunk that was missing on the loch-side wall, but what was left gave an amateur histo-rian like myself a good idea of what it must have looked like in its hey-day. I entered the weed-filled interior and looked around. It was cool and quiet inside, like the old place was somehow holding its breath until someone came along to restore it again. The atmosphere was not creepy as such, merely saddened by years of neglect. I stood there for a few moments, enjoying the peace, and taking in every feature and stone. As I looked up through the gaping wound of its former roof, I suddenly heard a rustle to my right. Something was in here with me. Startled, I spun around just in time to see a large raven take off and make a hurried exit out of one of the windows. Heart beating madly, I exhaled and decided it was time to explore the rest of the old place.

A light breeze was coming off the water as I exited the tower and sauntered along an overgrown pathway towards the southern end of the complex. It was a lovely day, and I enjoyed the sunshine on my face. I knew I should have had a parasol to prevent my pale face from turning brown, but it was such a delicious feeling having that warmth on my skin that I did not care. The insects were droning through the wild flowers and weeds that grew in abundance within the old castle walls. The loch, which I spied through breaks in the walls, was glittering in the sunlight and all felt well with the world. I had just reached the older part of the castle when Duncan suddenly appeared from a gap in the curtain wall. My heart leapt into my mouth when I saw him. He was dressed in brown tweed trousers and a white shirt that was open at the chest, revealing a smattering of dark hairs and his silver chain. His feet were bare. He smiled, showing off a set of perfect white teeth.

'Hello Duncan,' I said. I suddenly felt shy and could feel a flush rise in my neck and spread all over my face.

'Miss Esther ,' he replied with a slight bow of his head. 'What are you doing here? Why aren't you with your master?'

'I have the day off. So, I thought I would explore the castle and surrounding area.'

'And what do you think so far?'

'It's beautiful here.' I looked around me, wistfully taking in the majesty of the scenery.

'Yes, it is.' His eyes bore into mine. 'I love it here. It is home.'

I looked at him, surprised. I thought gypsies were always on the move. It didn't occur to me that they might stay in one place. That was not my understanding of their culture.

'Would you like me to show you, my home?'

It was a question that was hard to answer. One part of me

wanted desperately to get to know him better and spend time with him. The other part was wary of strangers. What if he turned out to be bad?

'Yes, yes, I would.' It was out before I could stop it and I blushed again. I briefly wondered where the gypsy camp was. I had not seen any of them, but I reasoned it must be nearby, and I was prepared to run if things got uncomfortable. He seemed pleased with my answer.

We walked out of the castle complex and, Duncan leading, followed a rough path close to the loch, heading in a northerly direction. He was silent all the while, and I wondered about him. Who were his people? How did he live? He must have felt me looking at him, for he turned and gave me a smile that lit up his entire face. I smiled back, for how could I not? Solemn-faced, Duncan was handsome. Smiling, he was stunning.

'It is not much further,' he said in his soft Highland accent.

The going got rougher underfoot, and he put out his hand to help me. At first, I was reluctant to take it. This man was a stranger to me. I should not do it, but something about his genial manner and honest face told me it would be alright. I held his hand; it was rough, the hand of a working man, and warm.

'Thank you.'

He gave me another smile that melted my heart and, hand-in-hand, we walked up the hill. The path led into a small group of trees and suddenly this plan of mine didn't seem such a good idea. I hesitated. He looked at me and frowned.

'Why have you stopped?'

'I…' How could I tell him that I thought I was putting myself in danger?

'You will be safe, I promise.'

I looked into those dark brown eyes and felt that what he

said would be true. I took a deep breath. I had already come so far and something about him made me feel safe.

'Alright.'

He led me through the trees until we came to a group of gorse bushes sitting in amongst large boulders on the hillside. He took me behind one bush to a hidden cave opening that was just big enough and wide enough to admit an adult human. Without hesitating, he let go of my hand and entered. Still not sure I was doing the sensible thing; I pushed all doubts of my mind and followed him.

The cave was dim, the only brightness coming from the opening, but as my eyes adjusted to the light, I could see that the cave was more like a tunnel and he was at the other end of it, beckoning me to follow.

The tunnel had been hewn out by hand, going by the pick marks on the walls and led into a dark cave. As he went around the carved room lighting candles, I began to see that this was his main living area. There were handmade wooden chairs positioned around a small wooden dining table in front of a black metal stove, its chimney rising up and out the ceiling of the cavern. It must have been lit, for the cave was warm and cosy. A large wooden bed lay in one corner, covered in sheepskins and wool blankets. A pile of books sat next to a brass candlestick on an old wooden box that had been upturned to make a table. On the right of the bed was another doorway covered by what looked like an old sailcloth. I wondered where it led to.

'Come and sit. I'll make you some tea.' He finished lighting the last candle and got to work on the stove. He filled an old black kettle with fresh water that was running in a steady stream down the wall close to the table and placed it on top of the stove. Fetching a teapot from a small cupboard at the side of the stove, he spooned loose tea into it from a tea tin sitting on the side.

'I don't have any milk. Do you take milk in your tea?' he asked apologetically.

'No, black is fine,' I replied, still looking around me. There were a few frayed posters attached to the walls, and the floor appeared to be soil covered with plaited rushes.

'Do you like my home?' he asked as he placed two porcelain cups on the table.

'It's lovely,' I replied.

'I know it's probably not what you are used to, but it does me.'

'I don't know who you think I am, Duncan, but I didn't grow up rich,' I replied. 'My father is a farmhand and my mother takes in washing. We don't have a lot of money and I have five brothers and sisters.'

'Is that why you are working for your master? Because you are poor?'

'That, and I wanted a bit of adventure,' I admitted.

'I understand.' He poured the now boiling water into the teapot and gave it a stir. He then brought it to the table.

It was my turn to ask the questions. 'So, how long have you lived here? I thought you might have been a… a… traveller.' I didn't want to use the word for fear it might insult him.

He smiled. 'A gypsy, you mean?'

'Well, yes.'

'No. I'm not a gypsy. My family and I have lived in these parts for generations.'

'Ah. I'm sorry. It was just something Cassius said.'

'Cassius?'

'The dwarf who works for Dr . Dwell.'

He poured me tea in silence. Then he said: 'This Dr . Dwell worries me. Do you know how long he intends to be in this area?'

I did not know and told him so. 'I don't think he intended to be here for long, but as every day passes, he grows more and more determined to catch the monster. I think he will stay until he finds it.'

'Well, that's worrying. I cannot keep them locked up indefinitely.' He took a sip of his tea and frowned.

'Can't keep who locked up?'

He leant across the table and touched my hand. It felt like electricity coursed through me. I looked away.

'Can I trust you?'

I looked up. His eyes were so full of hope they would have melted the hardest of hearts. 'Yes, of course you can.'

'Alright, follow me.'

He put his cup down on the table, rose, and put his hand out to me. Nervously, I stood up and took it. He led me towards the makeshift sailcloth door and pulled it aside. An icy draught blew over me and made me shiver. Pausing only to lift the candle from his bedside table, he plunged into the darkness, the light from it dancing in shadows on the hand-hewn walls, pulling me in with him.

We walked in silence for a minute or so before reaching the top of a short flight of shallow stairs. As we descended, Duncan paused every few seconds to make sure I was negotiating them with care. We walked for a few moments before coming out into a large, echoing cavern. I shivered and watched as he left me in the darkness for a few moments to light a series of oil lamps placed strategically along the cave wall. As he lit the one furthest away, it became clear to me that this cave was so cold because most of it was underwater. Loch water to be precise. It glittered under the soft lamplight.

'Loch Ness,' he said by way of explanation.

'So, who have we come to see?' Curiosity was getting the better of me. I looked around and could see no-one.

'One moment.' He handed me the candlestick, placed his forefinger and thumb into his mouth, and let out a loud whistle. In a dark corner of the cave, I could hear something big slide into the water. I immediately turned to where the noise had come from. Nervous, but unable to look away, I watched as the light began to pick out a shape in the water. As it grew closer, I could see it was being followed by more shapes. Then the first creature surfaced, and I gasped. It was an aquatic animal with a large head and a long, slim neck. As it came to the shallower part of the water, I made out a long tail and four flippers. It was about the size of a walrus and had greyish skin, a face with large soft brown eyes and a long snout.

'It's the… it's the…' So astonished was I that I could not get the words out.

# Chapter 5

The Loch Ness Monster? Yes. Well, one of them.'
'There's more?'
Sure enough, behind the first one were three more, each slightly smaller than the one before it.

'It's real. They're real.' I clasped my hand to my mouth and watched as they began to shuffle up on to the shore.

'Yes. Would you like to meet them?'

He slowly and carefully walked towards the biggest of the creatures. He put out a hand and the nearest creature moved forward to nuzzle it with its noble grey head.

'This one I call Athair. It means father in Gaelic. He is the leader of the group.' He stroked the creature's smooth muzzle, and it licked him. 'Come over and meet him.'

I will not lie, I was terrified at first. I had never seen such a prehistoric creature before and I was frightened it would harm me. But Duncan reassured me I would be perfectly safe, that the creature was harmless. He instructed me how to approach them, how to stand, and when to stretch out my hand. Before I knew it, I was also patting the beautiful, elusive creature. It felt soft and warm, the way I always imagined a seal to feel. In fact, its coat very much resembled that of the grey seals I had often seen in and around my Ayrshire home. This wasn't a reptile at all, but some sort of mystical mammal.

'This is wonderful, I said breathlessly. I could barely contain my excitement. 'The Loch Ness monster exists and there is a whole family of them. It is truly amazing.'

'Yes, but you must never tell a living soul of what you have seen,' he warned. 'Promise me you won't say a word to anyone, especially your master. I cannot keep them safe if people know about them. They will want to study them and my friends will have no peace.'

I promised. He smiled, and I felt a rush of something I had never felt before. It was excitement and longing and fear all wrapped up into one overwhelming feeling. Was I attracted to Duncan? The thought both surprised and delighted me, but mixed around it was anxiety. What if he didn't like me? What could I possibly hope to happen? Was it even proper? I could not draw my eyes away from Duncan's handsome face and he was looking at me strangely, intensely, like at any moment he might lean forward and kiss me passionately on my mouth. How I longed for him to kiss me. Then, as quick as a flash, Duncan looked away, and the moment was lost.

'Your tea will be getting cold,' he said and moved off in the direction of the stairs.

Disappointed, I followed him back up to his apartment and sat down at the dining table. In silence, I picked up my cup and took a sip. The tea was sweet and delicious and I wondered what it was made of. It certainly wasn't the tea I was used to, but something else.

'May I ask a favour of you?' Duncan asked, cutting into my thoughts.

'Yes, of course.'

'I must protect my friends. They are the last of their species. If they were to be taken into captivity or killed, it would be devastating. Will you help me? Will you keep me informed as to Dwell's intentions?'

'He doesn't share such details with me.'

'But anything you see or hear that you think I should know, will you tell me?'

'Yes, of course.' I said it without hesitation, for in my heart of hearts I firmly believed Dwell intended on harming them and said so.

'It is as I feared,' he replied. He drained his cup. 'I think it's time you went back,' he said. 'They might be getting worried about you.'

'I doubt that. Dwell went on the loch without me today.'

'He is there hunting them now?' He was alarmed.

'Yes.'

'I must go and see what he's doing. Please, you must leave now. I will see you out.'

I wanted to stay longer, to be with him some more, but readily agreed. I could see how anxious he had become. I thanked him for the tea and he showed me out of the cave. Giving me instructions on how to get back to the castle, he bid me farewell and disappeared back inside.

Unsure how to feel about this extraordinary encounter, I hurried back through the trees and re-joined the path to the castle. I turned around to see if Duncan had re-emerged, but he was not there.

I did not see Duncan for the whole of the next day. However, Dwell did ask me to accompany him on the little puffer again. He was even courteous when he took my hand and helped me board the little steamboat. I wondered at his change of attitude towards me, but decided to say nothing. It would not do to get on his wrong side. He was paying me, after all. I was here to work for him. And I could watch over what he was doing, learn what he was planning, while I was at it.

Dwell was in a fine mood as the little boat moved away from the dock. He joked and smiled at the captain. He called the engineer a 'capital fellow' and offered me a shot of rum from his own flask. I declined, but thanked him warmly. As we made our way up the loch, the few clouds in the sky dissipated, allowing the warm summer sun to sparkle and play on the tiny waves that lapped against the bow. The water was a dark navy blue scudded with little white ripples blown up by a slight breeze. The mountains were green and purple, reaching up to the sky like the tips of giant fingers on an upturned enormous hand. Along the loch, dotted here and there, were clumps of dark green fir trees, their branches reaching out in homage to the wonderful day it was already promising to be. I took a seat at the prow of the boat and enjoyed the gentle puff-puff of its engines as it slowly cut through the languid water, making its way to Fort Augustus on the south-west tip of the loch. I smiled to myself, knowing full well that Duncan had hidden the creatures in a cave near our base and that Dwell would be nowhere near them for today at least.

'What are you so happy about?' Dwell asked, stumbling across one of the wooden boxes he had his equipment stashed in. He huffed as he moved the box out of the way.

'It's such a lovely day and I'm so pleased to be here; I can't help but smile.'

'Yes, it is a splendid day.' He took a sip from his flask.

'Shall we be searching all day, Dr . Dwell?' I hoped my question wouldn't raise his suspicions. He wasn't a stupid man.

He turned to me and frowned. 'Aren't you enjoying yourself, Miss Abercrombie.'

'I am, very much so, Dr . Dwell, I just wondered, that is all.' I gave him my sweetest of smiles.

'Well, actually, now that you have raised the issue, we will in fact only be on the loch for the morning. I need to retrieve some listening equipment I left in the water last night. I'm hoping to have picked up some sounds of activity from last night.'

'Well, I hope it has picked up something,' I replied as gaily as I could. I did not want him suspecting I was working against him.

He said nothing else to me for the rest of that morning, so caught up was he in retrieving his equipment. So, I spent the voyage happily watching for Duncan in the loch. I don't know why, but at the time it was never strange to me that this handsome Highlander would spend so much time in the freezing waters of Loch Ness. I had just assumed he enjoyed swimming. I scanned the loch-side, hoping to see him, but to no avail... but, I did see something odd.

Dwell was fiddling with old whisky barrels he was using as floats to mark where his equipment was submerged. He was hanging over the side of the puffer, adjusting the rope and muttering to himself. Bored, I was watching him and happened to glance off in the distance behind him when something caught me eye. What is that? I stood up and walked towards him to get a better look. On a tiny island, laden with spindly trees, the large black horse from before stood staring at me. As I watched it, it turned its back and went into the water, disappearing under the dark waves. I waited to see where it would resurface, but could not find it.

'What are you looking at?' Captain Buchan was at my back. He smelled of engine oil and tobacco.

'I thought I saw…'

'A Cherry Island,' he said, recognising the small patch of land. 'The locals here think it's magical,' he added. 'It's man-made, you know? Created by men from long ago as a place to lay their dead.'

I turned to look at him. 'Is it magical?'

He waved a hand. 'That's just folklore. There's no magic on that island, just trees.'

'And are those cherry trees on there?'

He shrugged. 'No idea, but it's a pretty name for such a small island, isn't it?'

I looked once more to where the horse had been, but it had gone. I returned to my spot on the deck, unnerved by its disappearance. What if it had drowned? Dwell calling my name broke into my thoughts.

'Come and give us a hand, young lady!' He shouted from the prow. He was standing with the captain, engineer and the mate attempting to haul his listening device on board. They were struggling. I ran to their aid. I was only a slip of a girl, but everything helps, I suppose. We heaved the heavy, dripping instrument aboard and Dwell quickly righted it. He looked extremely pleased with himself as he inspected its panel.

'Yes, I think we might have something.'

My stomach twisted at his words. Surely, Duncan had kept the creatures inside? Surely, none had got out to make subaqueous noises? Dwell turned to the captain.

'Take us back to shore, Captain. I need to inspect what we have on this recording.'

After we disembarked, I did not see Dwell again for the rest of the day. Cassius claimed he was too busy tweaking his invention to be bothered with a chit of girl like me.

'Do you know if he's planning on going out on the loch again?' I asked, watching the little man as he sorted through a large wooden toolkit. I was standing at the door of the barn, looking out over the loch, and did not notice the effect that the question had had on him.

'Why do you want to know?'

I turned around to see Cassius staring at me, wrench in hand. I suddenly felt uncomfortable.

'Well,' I began. 'I was hoping to have the afternoon to myself. I thought I might like to go for a walk or get a lift to Fort Augustus for shopping.'

He appeared to be satisfied with my explanation, but not with what he was doing. He threw the wrench into the box with a clang. Wiping his hands on his leather apron, he walked up to me and then smiled. Although the smile danced about his lips, it did not meet his eyes.

'So, you want to go shopping?'

'Yes.'

'How about I take you in one of the steam carriages?'

'That would be wonderful.'

'I'm not going to Fort Augustus though '

'Oh. Well, that's okay. I'll go shopping another day.'

'No, please join me. I could do with the company,' he said with a salacious smile. 'Besides, I'm going to pick something up for Dr . Dwell that I'm sure you'll approve of.'

'I will? What is it?' Not another weapon, surely?

'It's a secret.' He tapped his nose with a finger.

I took a step closer to him and said conspiratorially: 'But surely you can tell me? I'm part of the team.'

He looked at me as if sizing me up. Then he looked out of the barn doors, seeking anyone who might overhear. 'Alright,' he said, 'I'll tell you, but only if you accompany me to go and fetch it.'

Having no other option and burning with curiosity, I agreed.

Half an hour later, I was sitting in the splendid comfort of the steam carriage with Cassius up front, driving. It was a fine afternoon, so I put the window down and enjoyed the sweet smell of wild flowers as we made our way along the single-track roads heading north.

'So, where are we going?' I shouted as we trailed the side of the loch. It was looking really beautiful today. The sunlight was sparkling on the still water. Some birds swooped and played amongst the trees and, on the mountainside, sheep and Highland cattle grazed in peaceful harmony. Cassius did not answer, but I could hear him cackling loudly on his perch at the front of the carriage.

We arrived at Beauly railway station three-and-a-half hours after leaving Strone. By that point, I was numb from sitting so long on the horsehair stuffed seats and where I was not numb; I was stiff and sore. I regretted agreeing to come on this journey, but the desire to see what Dwell had in store next was too great. I had to know what he was planning.

The carriage drew up outside the station and Cassius jumped down. His craggy face appeared at the window, giving me a start.

'Are you coming?' he asked.

I nodded and got out of the carriage.

The railway station had been built 27 years before and was beautifully kept. The station house had window boxes at every window, full of summer blooms and scents. The station master, sporting a large handlebar moustache, was standing at the platform looking from his pocket watch to a point somewhere up the line, and then back again. He frowned as we approached.

'The train is running late,' he told us gruffly. 'It's normally bang on time, but something must have delayed it. Are you going far?'

'We're actually here to pick something up,' Cassius informed him.

'Oh, aye? Well, it'll be here any minute.' He gave us a quick nod before walking away towards the ticket office.

Cassius gave me a wink and went to sit on a bench that backed on to the station house.

'Are you going to stand there growing tall or are you coming to sit by me?' he asked. 'We could be awhile yet. These Highland trains often have problems with landslides and cows on the line and the like.'

I looked up the line, saw no sign of the train, and joined him. We sat there, the pair of us, unable or unwilling to engage in any small talk. I, for one, found my tongue tied. I could not think of a single thing to say to my companion other than enquire after his health. Cassius gave me a sharp look before confirming what I already knew, that he was in perfect health.

'What are you asking me that for, girl?' he growled. 'Haven't you got a better conversation than that?'

'Well, I don't see you contributing anything.' It was out before I could stop it. My mother had always said I was prone to speak without thinking, and this just proved it. He glared at me and was about to retort when a train whistle could be heard in the distance. As one, we got to our feet and peered down the line. I could just make out the white plumes of smoke filtering through the trees. The train was coming.

Cassius could hardly contain his excitement as a huge black

steam train rounded the corner and chuffed towards us, dragging its green carriages behind it. The little man danced from foot to foot impatiently as the train slowed and pulled into the tiny station. As it stopped, a porter hurried out of the station house and took up position next to the first carriage. Although it pulled three carriages, there was only room for passengers to disembark from one, and only one person did that: a large man wearing a black homburg hat and wearing a long black cloak over his suit. He got down from the carriage, dragging a small trunk behind him, and shouted for the porter to retrieve his boxes from the carriage. It was only then that he spied Cassius, and a grin broke over his face.

'Ironblood! You old son of a gun!' he cried, dumping his trunk on the platform and walking, with open arms, towards the dwarf. Cassius beamed in return and went in for a hug. From where I was standing, it looked like a father hugging his child. 'How are you? And where is Dwell?' It was then that he noticed me, and a leering smile spread over his ruddy face.

'He's back at base. He says he'll see you for a drink in the bar!' Cassius said.

'Never mind that! Who is the luscious bit of skirt?' He strode over to me and put out a hand. Reluctantly, I offered my own and shuddered when he bent down to kiss my hand. I felt the warm wet lips land on the back of my hand, the tongue lick me. He kept a hold of it as I tried to pull away and raised his head. 'So, what do they call you?'

'Miss Esther Abercrombie, sir.'

'Well, Miss Abercrombie, it is an absolute delight to meet you. I look forward to getting better acquainted.'

And you are? I wanted to say, but held my tongue. I looked at Cassius. Introduce me, I tried to convey. He got it right away.

LOCHNESS

'Miss Abercrombie, this is my great friend, Charles Warrington.'

'Indeed, that is my name!' The big man said. 'Big game hunter and whaler extraordinaire.'

A polite cough sounded behind him and Warrington turned to find the ticket collector standing next to large wooden boxes. His face was red and there was sweat dripping down his forehead from the exertion of removing them from the carriage.

'Your boxes, sir.'

'Ah, yes!' Warrington reached into a jacket pocket and pulled out some coins. He gave one to the porter. 'Thank you, my good man.' He turned to Cassius. 'So, where's this steam carriage Dwell is always bragging about? Is it as good as he says?'

'Better.'

They were about to walk away when the poor porter shouted after them. 'Gentlemen! Your boxes!'

Warrington looked over one great shoulder. 'Put them in the carriage for me, will you? There's a good man.'

The porter looked at the hunter in dismay and then down at the boxes.

'Can I help you?' I offered.

'No, miss, that's all right. I'll just get my cart and use that.'

Warrington insisted on sitting up front on the driver's box with Cassius. His luggage deemed too precious to be strapped to the back of the carriage or on the roof, so was placed inside. I was to squeeze in as best I could. It was not a comfortable journey back and the two men ignored me for the duration. From my position scrunched up against the interior wall of the carriage, fearful a box would fall on me, I could hear them laughing and reminiscing about past adventures. It irked me somewhat, but I tried to have some dignity about me. At least I could sit and think on the way home without interruption. I wondered who this Warrington was and what was in his boxes. More weapons, I assumed. He had said he was a Big Game Hunter and whaler. That meant Dwell had brought him here to help in the hunt for the monsters. I had to tell Duncan as soon as we got back.

# Chapter 6

We arrived back at the inn around 7pm, just in time for dinner, and found Dwell standing outside smoking his pipe. From the carriage, I could see his joy as he saw us approaching. He had suddenly become more animated, waving his arms in the air and shouting 'Halloo'. Warrington evidently meant a great deal to him, and this belief was confirmed when Warrington jumped down from his seat before the carriage had even stopped and rushed into Dwell's arms. The two men hugged and patted each other on the back like lifelong friends.

'Warrington! So good to see you. How long's it been?' Dwell's distinctive baritone found its way to me in the carriage.

'Too long, old friend, too long…'

Their voices drifted away as the two men walked away arm-in-arm and entered the inn, leaving Cassius and myself with Warrington's things. I struggled to open the carriage door and release myself from the claustrophobic interior. I stepped down from the carriage and breathed in the fresh evening air. Cassius climbed down from the driver's box and unloaded the wooden boxes.

'May I help, Mr. Ironblood?' I asked. I felt sorry for him always being left to do everything himself. He looked at me like I was crazy.

'No thank you, Miss Abercrombie, I'm quite able to unload the carriage by myself.'

'I didn't mean…' I began, but the little man ignored me and got on with his work.

I left him to it and entered the inn to seek some supper. Dwell and Warrington were sitting at a table in front of the fire, drinking from tankards of ale. Warrington was furnishing Dwell with his latest adventures and neither looked at me as I walked towards them. Realising I was being purposely ignored, I made my way to the bar and asked Mrs. Mackintosh if I might have some supper.

'Yes, I have some stew left, lass,' she replied. 'I tell you what, why don't you come in the back and sup with me? Leave the gentlemen to their ale. Adam, take over, will you? I'll give you a shout when the gentlemen's dinner is ready to be put out.' The boy nodded. His mother lifted the hatch on the counter and bade me follow her inside.

We went into a small neat parlour. Mrs. Mackintosh invited me to sit on the sofa whilst she went to fetch our food. I looked around the room while I waited. It was beautifully kept with its pristine, white-washed walls and well-swept stone floors. Apart from the sofa, there were also two armchairs carefully placed on either side of a small fireplace, and rugs had been laid beneath them, which gave the room a cosy feel. Above the mantel, twin china dog statues sat either end beneath candlesticks and in the centre was a framed photograph of a man and woman on their wedding day. The woman was obviously Mrs. Mackintosh in her younger days. The man I assumed to be her husband.

Neither were smiling, as was the fashion in those days, but by the way he was staring proudly out of that image, I could see Mr. Mackintosh was delighted with his catch. Above the mantel was a framed black-and-white photograph of a loch and some mountains. I recognised it immediately as Loch Ness. To the left of the fire, standing proud against the wall, was a grandfather clock gently ticking away.

My hostess returned some minutes later with a wooden tray laden with a bowl, cutlery and a glass of port. The smell of beef stew filled my nostrils and my mouth burst with saliva. I was hungrier than I had thought. She handed me the tray and disappeared again. Seconds later, she was back with her own tray. She sat down on one of the armchairs and settled the tray on her knee. She looked at me.

'Well, aren't you eating, girl?'

I smiled and took up my fork . I daintily placed some food in my mouth and ate. It was delicious. Flavour washed over my tastebuds.

'It's good?' she wanted to know.

I nodded; mouth still full. 'Yes,' I replied when I finally swallowed.

'So, how are you and Dr . Dwell getting on with finding the monster?' she asked between mouthfuls. I looked at her, unsure of how to answer. 'Oh, was it supposed to be a secret?' She laughed. 'Nothing's ever a secret around here'

'It's not going as well as Dr . Dwell had hoped,' I replied diplomatically. 'He can't seem to find the creature.' I must have smiled slightly then, for her eyes narrowed.

'And this new man, do you think he'll be able to find them… it?'

If she hoped I hadn't picked up on that small misstep, she

was mistaken. She looked at me, her eyes fearful I had noticed.
I didn't acknowledge it.

'Yes, I believe Mr. Warrington is some sort of Big Game
Hunter,' I said.

'So, they do mean to capture and kill the creature, then?' She
was genuinely concerned.

I put my fork down. 'Not if I have anything to do with it,
Mrs. Mackintosh.'

She smiled, relief blossoming in her eyes. 'Good, good,' she
said. 'I knew you were a decent one. I told Duncan that only
Yesterday.'

I jumped on that as soon as I heard his name. 'You know
Duncan?'

'Everyone around here knows Duncan… and his family. They are part of the landscape. Why, without them…' She
looked away. Her hand flew to her chin, and she rubbed it
thoughtfully. 'No, I've said too much. It's up to him to tell you.'

'Tell me what?'

But she would not be drawn on the subject and instead
talked about the history of the inn and her late husband's connection to it. His family had been there for several generations,
as long as anyone could remember. She, herself, was from nearby Drumnadrochit, the daughter of a carter. She spoke about
their courting days and her marriage.

'Then we were blessed with our Adam,' she said proudly.
'He's always been such a wonderful help to me.' Her demeanour
darkened. 'Five years ago, Rab became sick and died. The doctor
said it was dropsy, but I don't know. I think it was his indolence
and the drink that finally took him. He is no loss; I can tell you.'
She smiled. 'It's just been me and the boy ever since.'

Just then the grandfather clock chimed the half hour, and

Mrs. Mackintosh started. She glanced around at it.

'Goodness, look at the time! I need to get back to the bar.' She stood up and looked at me. 'Finish up, lass. You'll be wanting to go warn Duncan of the Big Game Hunter, I suppose?'

'Yes, how did you know?'

'I can see it in your eyes that you are no fan of what Dr . Dwell proposes.'

'If you know what he's planning to do, why do you let us still stay here?' I asked.

She smiled. 'I always think it's better to keep your enemies close by so that you know what they are getting up to. If I turned you all out, how would I be able to keep track of you all?'

'You've been spying on us?' I was shocked. She always seemed so nice.

'Not as such,' she replied. 'Our creatures are sacred to our lands, and I don't just mean the one Dwell is chasing. Without them, Loch Ness would not be the magical place it is. It's important to me and to everyone who lives here that we safeguard them all. So, we always keep a watchful eye on visitors. It's just what we do.' She walked over to the door. 'Besides, I have to make a living!' With that last quip, she disappeared, leaving me to mull over her words.

So, I thought, the Loch Ness Monsters weren't the only unusual creatures around here. I wondered what else this land hid.

I did not sit long in the drawing room, but finished my food and returned the tray to the kitchen.

'You know you don't have to go out through the bar,' she said, nodding towards a plain wooden door at the rear of the kitchen.

'Thank you, Mrs. Mackintosh.'

Duncan was standing near the pier, looking out over the

loch, when I approached. Tall and handsome, it was hard not to admire him, but I was not there for romance. I had information to impart. He turned as I approached; a broad smile spread out over his beautiful face.

'Miss Esther Abercrombie,' he said and gave a small bow, causing me to smile. 'You look lovely tonight.'

Well, that was a lie. I knew that. For I had been travelling in the carriage for most of the day and felt dishevelled and unclean. However, I appreciated his compliment and thanked him. Then I grew serious.

'Duncan, may we walk somewhere? I have some important news to tell you,' I said in a low voice.

He nodded and offered me his arm. Looking around to make sure we had not been seen, I took it and together we walked away from the pier towards the ruins of Urquhart Castle. I wish now I had been more thorough that evening, for it was only later that I discovered that far from sneaking off as I had hoped, someone had seen us leave and that would have consequences for us later.

However, oblivious to the danger, I allowed Duncan to escort me to the ruins before telling him about my afternoon travels and the danger Charles Warrington posed to the creatures.

'Can you find out what he plans to do?' Duncan asked as we sat on a curtain wall of the castle and watched the sun set over the mountains. The sunset was throwing up all manner of colours—oranges, yellows, reds, blues and greens – and it was hard not to be distracted by the romance of this wonderful show. 'If you're able, find out what is in his boxes.'

'I tried to look earlier when I was in the carriage, but they were nailed shut.' We fell into a companionable silence for a few moments, each lost in our own thoughts. I found myself

wishing that circumstances were different, that we were courting and that this was just a romantic evening with the man of
my dreams. However, I wasn't there for love. We did not have
that type of relationship, no matter how much I wished it, and I
would just have to deal with that. Suddenly Duncan started and
I swear I thought one of his ears moved. He put his fingers to
his lips so that I would remain silent and mimed that he thought
someone was listening.

'So, pray tell Miss Abercrombie, what's it like growing up
on a farm?' he asked loud enough for whoever or whatever was
hiding nearby, and encouraged me to answer.

'It is hard work,' I replied, 'but thankfully I have plenty of
brothers and sisters to help my mother and father.'

Duncan slid off the wall and crept away in the opposite direction to where he had indicated someone was hiding. I frowned,
but did not give him away.

'And do you have a sweetheart where you come from?'

'There was a boy who once said he liked me,' I said, watching
him creep around to the corner of the wall. Duncan turned and
gave me a sharp look, 'but I did not feel the same way about
him. Of course, I will have to marry at some point, but I really
wanted to see a bit more of the world.' He motioned to me
to turn back around and look at the loch. I should not look at
him. 'That's why I applied for the position with Dr . Dwell. As a
prominent cryptozoologist, he travels the world, you see, and I
thought it would be a marvellous thing to do. Of course, I have
only gotten as far as Loch Ness, but I really hope Dr . Dwell will
continue my employment and take me to Africa… or China…
or Australia…'

A loud squeak and rustling in the undergrowth interrupted
my speech. Then the familiar voice of Cassius Ironblood rang

out: 'Unhand me, you scoundrel!'

I turned around to see a grinning Duncan striding back towards me with Cassius tucked safely under his arm. The dwarf was kicking and hitting and shouting expletives and threats.

'Come and see who was spying on us in the bushes,' Duncan said, as he righted the little man and placed him gently on the ground. Cassius brushed himself down before scowling at his captor.

'I'll have you know I was not spying on you,' he began. 'I just happened to be taking a walk when I followed the path along to the castle. I have not yet explored the ruins, and I thought it would be an interesting thing to do. Then you appeared from nowhere, lifted me off my feet and carried me here!' There was genuine indignation in his voice and he looked so comical standing there looking furious that I had to stifle a laugh. He turned around and gave me a hard stare. 'Are you laughing at me? Is it funny that someone of my stature can easily be picked up and carted around? Does that make you giggle, Miss Abercrombie? Because I don't find it funny, not one little bit. I have enough trouble with humans treating me as something lesser without some great big hulking… creature like him picking me up.'

'Well, you shouldn't have been spying on us,' Duncan replied. He crossed his arms and stood looking at Cassius.

'I told you I was not…'

'Then why were you hiding in the bushes?'

That was a question Cassius could not answer. He looked away from Duncan then and stared at the pretty flowering wild flowers growing in great clumps either side of the path.

'Well, I…' He looked at me. 'I… wouldn't like to say what I was doing there. It's not for the ears of young ladies!'

'Look, just admit it,' Duncan continued. 'You were following us to see what we were doing. That makes you a voyeur.'

Cassius pressed his lips together and looked at Duncan with disgust. 'I was not spying, I was merely ensuring Miss Abercrombie was safe,' he said at last.

'I'm perfectly safe, Mr. Ironblood,' I said, getting to my feet and walking towards them. 'Mr.... er... Duncan here was just showing me the castle and telling me its history. It was quite interesting,' I lied.

'Well, it's not seemly for a young woman like you to go walking out with a young man like... him!' The dwarf jerked his head in Duncan's direction. 'It's not right.' Then he got all fatherly. 'It's getting late, Miss Abercrombie Please allow me to escort you back to the inn.'

'I am quite happy here, Mr. Ironblood, and my friend will escort me back.'

'Indeed, he will not! You have already overstepped the mark by walking out with him, Miss Abercrombie. Do I have to fetch Dr . Dwell and tell him what is going on? You have already fallen out of favour; I would not like to have to give him more bad news about your character!'

'Of all the...!' Duncan began, but I pitched in. I knew he was right. If Dwell were to hear of my indiscretion, he was sure to sack me right there and then. I couldn't afford to lose the job, not when I needed to find out what he was planning with Warrington.

'Mr. Ironblood... Cassius... that won't be necessary. I will return with you,' I said. I gave Duncan a smile and put out my hand. He took it and we shook. 'Thank you for the very interesting history talk on the castle. I hope that we can meet again soon.'

'My pleasure,' he said. His eyes gave me a quizzical look, but

I continued with my actions. I turned to Cassius.

'Mr. Ironblood, would you do me the honour of escorting me back to the inn?'

'Of course,' the dwarf replied, and he gave Duncan a look of satisfaction.

We had only walked some 20 feet when I suddenly remembered something. I stopped. Cassius looked up at me, puzzled.

'Oh!' I said, feigning womanly silliness. I took a plain white handkerchief from my pocket. 'I forgot to return my friend's handkerchief. Will you excuse me for a moment while I return it?'

The dwarf nodded like he wasn't sure whether to believe me, but Duncan was only a few feet away. How could he possibly protest? I hurried over and gave him the handkerchief. He looked at me, puzzled as to why I was giving him my own property.

'Take it,' I whispered. Then loudly I said: 'I forgot to return this, please accept my apology.'

'No matter at all, Miss Abercrombie,' he countered, taking the small square of cotton.

'I'll sneak down to the barn tonight after dark to see if I can find out what's in the boxes,' I whispered.

'I will meet you there,' he replied.

We both said our goodbyes again, and I returned to Cassius' side. I did not look back for fear the dwarf would suspect our camaraderie, but I could feel Duncan's brown eyes boring into my back. A thrilling shiver ran through my body as I thought of him and my heart felt full. He was always on my mind, filling my thoughts with his dark hair and handsome face. I secretly hoped he felt the same about me.

'What are you smiling at?' Cassius' voice broke into my daydream, bringing me back to Earth with a bump.

'What?'

'You have a stupid grin all over your face. It's not to do with that... that... creature back there, is it?' He demanded.

'Duncan is an amiable man,' I replied carefully.

'Yes, but you have a bit of a fancy for him, do you not?'

'No, most definitely I do not,' I lied, but in my heart, I knew I was falling for the handsome Highlander. I felt myself blush and hoped Cassius had not noticed.

'Well, watch your step, my girl. If Dr. Dwell finds out you're associating with strange men; he'll have you off this expedition as soon as you can say Loch Ness Monster!'

'I can assure you that we are mere acquaintances,' I said. He didn't look convinced.

'Hmmmph!'

Dwell and Warrington were still in the bar when we returned and were obviously drunk. Instead of the beer tankards I had left them with, they were now drinking the finest whisky from two crystal glasses and talking loudly about their joint venture ahead.

'Here's to us, Dwell!' Warrington bellowed. 'Here's to happy hunting tomorrow!'

'Yes, we'll track it down alright,' Dwell answered. Then he must have realised what he had said and that it might not have gone down well with the locals who were also in the bar. So, he added hastily: 'And I'll be able to study it at last!'

'Yeah! Study it!' Warrington echoed. He gave Dwell a wink. 'Here's to studying the creature!'

They clinked glasses and then both spied Cassius and me standing at the bar entrance.

'Ironblood!' Dwell shouted. 'Come and join us for a drink!'

The dwarf gave me a smug look and went to join his master.

'You too Miss Abercrombie! Let's get some whisky down you. Might warm you up a little bit!' Warrington belched.

'No thank you, Mr. Warrington,' I replied testily. 'I am going to retire for the night. Good night, gentlemen.'

I waited until after 11 before I snuck back downstairs again. Loud voices filtered out through the bar door and I recognised them immediately. Slowly, silently, I approached it and peeped through the gap between the door and the door sill. The bar was empty, save for Dwell, Cassius, and Warrington. Silhouetted against the fire, they were still drinking at the table where I'd left them. They were having a merry old time, saluting each other with filled whisky glasses before clinking them together and draining the contents. They did not notice me spying on them from the hallway, nor me wrapping my shawl around my shoulders before slipping out of the front door. Even though I had thought to bring a lantern with me, I did not light it for fear I should be seen from the windows of the inn. Instead, under the dim light of a waxing moon, I stumbled over to the dark hulk that was the barn and made my way to its doors. Taking a quick look around me, I tried to open them, but found them to be padlocked. I rattled the padlock in my frustration, somehow hoping it would spring open on its own, but it stayed firmly locked. Damnit!

'Do you need some help there?' I nearly jumped out of my skin and turned to find Duncan standing in the shadows. I knew it was him from his voice and the graceful way he moved when he stepped out into the faded moonlight.

'You startled me!' I hissed. 'I thought I had been discovered!'

'Apologies, ma'am, that was not my intention.' He joined me at the doors. A grin spread across his face. 'Allow me.'

Still, to this day, I don't know what Duncan did to break open that padlock. He seemed to just touch it and it sprang open of its own accord.

'How did you…?' I began, astonished that the lock opened so easily for him.

'Let's just say I have a knack for opening such things,' Duncan said. 'Let's get inside. Did you bring a lantern?'

I nodded, and we stepped into the gloomy barn. Duncan carefully closed the barn doors behind us as I lit the lantern. I told Duncan that Dwell and the other two were busy getting drunk in the inn and that I did not think they would bother us tonight.

'We should be careful none-the-less,' he said, looking around us. 'The window shutters are closed. That's good. At least then our light will not be seen from outside.' He held the lantern up and began to inspect Dwell's equipment. 'Now, which ones belong to Warrington?'

It took us a full ten minutes to locate the boxes. They had been stored at the back of the barn under a large, oil-stained tarpaulin. Someone had nailed the boxes shut, as I had informed Duncan, so we went about trying to find something we could prise them open with. I went to the workbench and located a screwdriver and hammer. Duncan put out his hand for them, but I ignored him, preferring to open the boxes myself. Looking bemused, he allowed me to try. I got the lid off the first box on the second attempt.

'I'm impressed,' he said. 'I never knew human women could be so resourceful. I thought you were all about embroidery and cooking.'

'Not all women like to do those things,' I said somewhat sniffily. I hated being thought of as incapable of doing things like this. 'But some of us grew up on a farm with a father and brothers, and some of us had to muck in when required and that included using tools. It wasn't just the boys my father taught how to use tools.'

'Still, it was impressive.'

We looked inside the box. It was packed to the gunnels with explosives. I looked at Duncan and his face had gone white. Surely, they weren't planning to blow the creatures up? I wanted to see what was in the other box and I roped Duncan into helping me shift the top box onto the floor. I opened the second box and inside was what looked like a fisherman's net, but made out of fine, but strong chain metal. A net tough enough to capture prehistoric creatures. Neither of us said anything for a moment.

'Do you think he's going to use this to create an explosion at one end of the loch in order to drive the creatures into the net? Dwell wants the creature in one piece. It's the only explanation that makes sense.'

'Well, he won't be able to do that if he has no dynamite,' Duncan replied. He began to look around him. 'See if you can find some sacks or something that we can fill with these explosives so that we can remove them from here. We need to get rid of this stuff, and fast.'

'What about the net?'

'Let's sort out the dynamite first and then we'll worry about that.'

'What about the tarpaulin? We could load the dynamite on to it and drag it out of the barn.'

'Good thinking.'

We were just laying the tarpaulin out on the floor when something crashed near the door of the barn. We froze. Then slowly I looked around to see that one of the barn doors had swung open. Apparently on its own. Duncan saw it too. He put his finger to his lips, and then tiptoed towards the entranceway. As I watched, he reached for the door and pulled it towards him, securing it shut with the internal sliding latch. Then something must have caught his eye, for he frowned and indicated that he was going to investigate the area of the barn that housed Dwell's collection of inventions and the automatons. He disappeared into the shadows.

'What are you doing here?' It was the last thing I heard him say before there was a groan and something fell to the ground.

'Duncan?' I called. 'Are you alright?'

There was silence.

'Duncan?'

Holding the lantern in front of me, I followed his steps and found him lying prone on the ground, eyes closed, unconscious. I put the lantern down and went to his aid. His head was bleeding, but he was breathing.

'Duncan! What hap…pened?' I felt a nasty smelling rag covering my mouth and nose. Then everything went black.

# Chapter 7

I awoke to the sound of a cockerel crowing somewhere nearby. I opened my eyes and blinked. I was sitting on the floor of the barn; a gag in my mouth and my hands tied behind my back. My feet had also been bound. I desperately looked around for Duncan and saw that he was lying nearby, still out of it, and had also been bound. I made as much noise as my gag allowed, trying desperately to wake my companion, but he did not stir. Just at that moment, the barn door burst open and a triumphant looking Dwell strode in.

'Well, well, well,' he said. 'You have gotten yourself into a pretty big mess, haven't you, Miss Abercrombie? When Cassius told me this morning that he had caught both of you trying to sabotage my hunting expedition, I was a little surprised. I did not think you had it in you.' He hunkered down and checked that my binds were still tight. 'Of course, what could I expect from a young lady like yourself who has been walking out with a local behind my back? That speaks volumes about your moral character.' I tried to protest, but I couldn't. 'No, no, don't give me your excuses. Mr. Ironblood here has told me all about it.' I looked behind Dwell to see the dwarf smiling smugly at me.

The little horror actually had the audacity to wave. 'I can't have someone like you ruining my reputation, Miss Abercrombie. It wouldn't do, it wouldn't do at all. So, when I have finished my preparations today, I will be asking Mrs. Mackintosh to fetch the local constable. He can deal with your dishonest ways.' He looked down at Duncan. 'As for your friend, here, well…' He turned around to look at Cassius, who was now grinning madly and brandishing a crowbar. 'I think Cassius would like to deal with him later.'

I tried to shout and scream at them. No! Don't hurt him! But the muzzle prevented me. The only effect my protests had was to prompt my two captors into fits of laughter. Then Dwell patted my head and called me a good girl.

He stood up, adjusted his coat and took a deep breath. 'Today's the day I make history,' he said to no-one in particular. Then he turned back to me. 'Farewell, Miss Abercrombie, I can quite categorically say you have been the worst assistant I have ever had.' At that, he turned on his heel and strode out of the barn, Cassius at his heels. The barn door clattered loudly in their wake.

Now what could I do? Duncan was out cold. I was bound hand and foot. And the creatures were in deadly danger.

The first thing I had to do was break these bonds, but how? I frantically looked around the barn, at the workbench, on the floor, under Dwell's equipment, but could see nothing that could help. I knew Cassius had previously left a set of knives out on the table, but could not get to my feet. So, I did what any other self-respecting farm girl would who grew up with brothers, and threw myself to the ground and rolled to the workbench. Somehow, rather shakily, I got myself to my feet. The knives were lying glinting in the morning light streaming through the high window of the barn. Good. I shuffled so that my back was to the bench and used my fingers to pick up a knife. They curled around the handle of one, but I struggled to hold it properly and dropped it. Unperturbed, I tried again, this time picking up a second lighter knife and gripped it tightly. Carefully, I began to saw through my bonds, praying I wouldn't cut through my own wrists while I was at it . The action caused the ropes to tighten and cut into my flesh, causing me pain, but I kept going, knowing I had to free us, knowing only we could save the creatures and whatever else lived in the loch. Saw, saw, saw. I kept going until I felt the ropes suddenly loosen. With a gasp of relief, I threw the knife back on the bench and pulled my arms around to the front. I rubbed my wrists, massaging the feeling back into them. Then I picked up the knife again and cut myself free of the ropes tying my ankles. The gag was the last thing to go, and once I had discarded that, I rushed to Duncan's side to check for signs of life. He was pale. The only bit of colour was the blood on a cut on his head, but he was breathing. His skin was cold and clammy, but he was alive. I quickly cut his ropes and rolled him on to his back.

'Duncan! Duncan!' I called, but he didn't stir. I shook him, rubbed his face. Anything I could think of to  bring him back. His eyes fluttered open, and he grimaced.

'What happened? I feel awful.'

'Cassius drugged us. I think he might have used ether,' I replied. It was the only thing I knew of that could fell someone the size of Duncan so easily. 'Do you think you can sit up?'

He moved slowly, sitting up in stages. He clasped his head where the gash was. 'Did I hurt myself?'

'I think you might have hit your head on something when you fell.'

He tried to get up, but was weak and woozy. He fell back to the ground. 'I don't feel so good.' He looked at me, his normally bright brown eyes dark with pain and suffering. 'I need to get back into the water. Take me to the water.'

'There will be time to wash later. We need to go and save the creatures first,' I reminded him.

'No, I can't do anything until I rejuvenate… in the… water.'

I looked at him and wondered what on Earth was going on? Why would someone need to go in the water? I could understand if he wanted to freshen up, but we were in an urgent situation, even now Dwell and Warrington were getting ready to go out on the loch. I hadn't heard the puffer start up yet, but I was sure it would wheeze into life soon.

'Water,' Duncan said again, this time weaker than before. His eyes were pleading with me. I nodded. Water. With great difficulty, he was a large man, I heaved him to his feet and supported him as he stumbled towards the barn door. The sun shone brightly as we stepped outside, temporarily blinding us as we walked out into the morning. It was a beautiful start to the day, but I could not enjoy it, so worried was I not just about the creatures, but about Duncan as well. In the bright daylight, I could see his skin was not just pale, it was starting to turn a mottled grey. Terrified he was dying, I guided him down to the little pier where the puffer was moored. I got him to the end of the wooden walkway and was about to help him gently into the water when he suddenly broke free from my grip and launched himself into a perfect dive. He disappeared under the still water and I watched anxiously for him to surface, which he did a few seconds later. His head burst through the water and he looked over at me joyfully. I smiled back. Then I saw his expression change into fear. Something or someone had caught his attention. With real urgency, he signalled for me to get off the jetty and hide somewhere nearby. I looked behind me to see Dwell and Cassius standing at the door of the inn. They were deep in conversation and appeared to be waiting for someone. Warrington, no doubt. As quick as a flash, I ran along the small jetty and behind a small copse of bushes and trees. I cocooned myself amongst the branches and leaves and looked back at the loch. Duncan was swimming towards me. Within a few seconds, dripping wet, he joined me in the bushes and together we watched and waited.

'We haven't missed them,' I whispered to him. He was crouched so close to me I could feel the cold of the water against my cheek. 'You're freezing,' I added.

'It's fine,' he replied. 'I feel better. That's all that matters. Watch out! Here they come.'

I craned around to see Dwell and the dwarf walk towards the jetty.

'What are we going to do? How are we going to stop them?'

'We'll think of something,' Duncan replied.

We watched as Dwell paused and then held an animated conversation with Cassius. He was gesticulating towards the barn.

'He's telling Cassius to get the dynamite,' I said. 'He'll find out we've escaped. We need to do something and we need to do it now.'

Duncan glanced at the puffer. 'That machine. How does it work?'

'The engine burns coal, the coal creates heat, the heat warms up water, and the water creates steam, which makes the engine work… at least, I think that's how it works. I'm not an engineer.'

'So, if we stop one part of the process working, we can stop it all?'

'I suppose so.'

He looked at me, and there was a mischievous look on his face. 'Keep watch, will you? Shout if any of them come any nearer.'

'What are you going to do?' I wanted to know.

'I'm going to stop this machine from working.' With that, he slipped away from me and entered the loch once more. He swam around the puffer and I did not see him again until his head and shoulders appeared on the bow of the boat. I watched as he hauled himself on board and then went into the engine room. Once he had disappeared from sight, I turned my attentions back on Dwell and Cassius. The dwarf was striding towards the barn. As he arrived, he paused and peered into the open door. We had forgotten to shut it. I watched him stealthily enter the building. A moment later, he reappeared, agitated and worried. He shouted to Dwell.

'They've gone, they've gone!'

'What?' The cryptozoologist broke into a run and joined Cassius at the barn. He, too, disappeared inside, reappearing moments later, looking furious.

'Find them! They can't have gone far!' he instructed his servant.

As Cassius hurried off in the direction of Urqhuart Castle, Dwell stormed back into the inn. By this time, Warrington was standing in the doorway. A quick discussion occurred between the two men, and then Warrington ran off in the opposite direction to the dwarf. Dwell then turned his attention to the puffer. He paused to stare at the little boat for a few moments.

What's he doing? I wondered. Then I saw him stride down the hill towards the pier. He's coming to check if we are here. I glanced over at the boat, but could see no sign of Duncan. What can I do to warn him? I wondered desperately. Being a bit of a tomboy growing up, I did just about everything my brothers did, so it was not difficult for me to produce a loud whistle. I stuck my thumb and forefinger into my mouth and blew. A shrill whistle pierced the air. I looked over at the puffer. No sign of Duncan. However, the noise had alerted Dwell, who then ran to the boat. I whistled again, this time sending out three loud shrills. Duncan's face appeared at the cabin door. I pointed to Dwell, who had now reached the jetty. Duncan took one look at him and then, quick as a flash, dived over the boat's side and into the loch. As he stealthily swam around the stern and made his way towards me, Dwell embarked and rushed panicking into the wheelhouse.

'Did you disable it?' I asked as Duncan waded out of the loch and joined me on the shore.

'I think so. I hope so.' He held up a piece of metal machinery that glittered in the sunlight.

'What will we do now?'

'There's only one thing that we can do,' he said. He took my hand and pulled me to my feet. 'Do you trust me, Esther Abercrombie?' He looked deep into my eyes and I knew I would trust this man with my life.

'Yes, I do.'

'Well, I trust you and it's time you found out who I really am.' He let go of my hand and stepped back. He slipped off his wet shirt and went to work on the buttons of his trousers.

'Now, hold on a minute, I'm not that kind of woman,' I protested.

He laughed. 'It's not what you think.' He slid the wet trousers over his hips, and I immediately turned my back to him. I felt the heat of embarrassment wash over my face. What was he doing?

Why was he undressing like this? We didn't have time for it. We had to get away.

'Alright,' Duncan said.

I turned around and came face-to-face with the large, handsome black horse I'd been seeing over the past few days. I looked under it and behind it for my friend.

'Duncan? Duncan, where are you?'

'Get on,' said the horse.

'What?' Was I hallucinating? Did the horse just speak?

'Get on my back. Come on, we're wasting time.'

I grabbed a hold of the horse's black mane and heaved myself on to its back. Before my leg had even touched the animal's back, it was off, running towards the castle like its tail was on fire. I heard a shout as we passed the boat and craned around to see Dwell standing on the deck, shaking his fist at us.

'Ironblood! Ironblood! They're getting away!'

The dwarf, who had been on the castle path, turned around. He saw us coming so ran over to meet us, hands up, urging us to stop, but the horse ploughed on past him, sending the little man spinning to the ground. The horse galloped on and soon we had left the inn area and were speeding towards the castle ruin. Without dropping pace, the horse skirted the ruins and ran up into the woodland heading towards Duncan's cave home.

We reached the cave mouth moments later and came to a halt just outside the hidden doorway. I slid off the panting beast's back. Unsure of what to do next, I stared at the horse. It seemed to be waiting for me to do something. Not knowing what it wanted and feeling awkward, I did what I thought best and slipped into Duncan's home.

'I'll just wait in here,' I said to the horse.

I walked inside, stopping in his apartment, and stood awkwardly in the middle of the room, looking at the bare walls. I did not want to sit as the host had not invited me to, so I stayed there and hoped Duncan would show up soon. And show up, he did.

I heard a noise in the passageway and turned around. I gasped. Duncan was standing there before me, naked. I spun away and studied the cold fireplace, desperately trying not to blush.

'Oh! I'm sorry!' I reddened to the roots of my scalp.

'Don't be,' he said. I heard him stride over to his bed. The clothes box at the bottom of his bed was opened and I heard him rustle inside. 'I'm not ashamed and neither should you be.' Something was pulled out of the chest. 'Besides, I'm sure this is something you've seen before. You did grow up with brothers.'

'I know,' I replied. 'But it's different… they were children the last time I saw them naked and… well, you're all…' I turned to look at him. He had a pair of trousers on and was pulling a shirt over his toned, tanned body. The sight of him made me giddy. '… grown up.'

I suddenly felt hot and a little faint, so I sat down on one of his chairs. He came to me immediately and knelt down beside me, his eyes full of concern.

'Are you feeling alright, Esther ?'

'It's just been a trying morning.' Then I took a deep breath and asked the question I had been wanting to ask ever since we had arrived. 'Is there something you need to tell me about the horse?'

He looked away from me and bit his lip.

'Duncan?'

'It's difficult to say.'

'I'm listening.'

'You might not like it when I tell you. You might be afraid.'

'Whatever you have to say, I promise you I'll stay. I'm not scared of you or whatever it is you're hiding.'

He looked at me earnestly. 'I want you to know that I never, ever thought about killing you.'

'What do you mean?'

'All the stories–about us–are not all true.'

'Alright, but who or what are you?'

He stood up and walked away from me, coming to stand with his hands on the mantelpiece, staring into the dark unlit chasm of the fireplace. 'I'm not supposed to tell, but I think you need to know.' Then something seemed to occur to him. He turned around. 'Look, the creatures are in danger. Can't we have this conversation later?'

I shook my head. 'No, I want to have it now. You're not human, are you?'

'No.'

'So, what are you?'

He rubbed his chin. 'Have you heard of kelpies ?'

'Yes, they're water spirits who often turn into large black horses and entice innocent travellers on to their backs. Then they take them into the water and drown them. They can also take human… form.' I gasped. 'Are you telling me you're a Kelpie ?'

'Yes.'

'But I thought they were extinct or a myth or something.'

'No, we're very much alive,' he said. He looked at me hopefully. 'My kin live in a settlement deep in the mountains overlooking the Moray Firth. That's where I grew up.'

'How many kin?'

'There were a few hundred when I left. I don't know how

many now.' His voice faltered and I could see the hurt in his eyes.

'Don't you see them anymore?'

He shook his head.

'Why is that?'

'It doesn't matter why it is. That is something for the past. What matters is what's happening right now. We must stop Dwell. The sabotage I did on the puffer won't keep him off the loch for long. They'll have a replacement in a day or two at the most.' He held out a hand. 'Come on, let's go down to the cave. I need to check they're alright.'

The creatures were happily playing in the water when we arrived at the underground loch. They stopped their play and looked at us curiously, their wide eyes glinting in the light of the lamps we had brought with us. There was a sudden splash and one after the other, they swam over. Duncan looked relieved and went to greet the largest one. He put out a hand, and it nuzzled it affectionately.

'Hello Athair,' he murmured, patting the gentle beast's head.

'Are they a family? Mother, father and children?'

'I think so.'

I stepped in beside him and the creature studied me. Gingerly, I too put out my hand and he bent forward and sniffed it. I could feel his breath tickling my palm. Then he nudged it with his nose and allowed me to pet him again.

'They are lovely,' I said, running my hand over the smooth velvety snout.

'Yes.' He beamed at me. He was delighted that I could see the beauty in the creatures, too. 'But I can't keep them cooped up in this cave forever. They should be free to swim in the loch and do what they wish without fear of being captured and killed.'

He sighed. 'I don't know what else to do about your Dr . Dwell.'

'He's not my anything,' I replied. 'You know, he is revered throughout the Empire as an expert on cryptozoology and rare creatures. People actually think he's a hero for discovering new species that were once thought to be mythological. They believe he's doing the world a favour by uncovering them, when in fact, it's all about the money and prestige. He doesn't care about these animals. When all this is over, I'm going to take my story to the newspapers. People need to know about the real Dr . Dwell.'

'Do you think they'll care?'

'They will when I've finished with them,' I promised him.

'But what do we do in the meantime? How do we stop him? We are just two people with no weapons and no idea about what to do next.'

'Then we need to get help,' I replied.

My plan was simple, but it would need Duncan's agreement to take it forward. I was sure I could gain the assistance of the local people, but Duncan had to do something too. I told him what I wanted from him and he immediately blocked it.

'No.' He stroked Athair's muzzle and would not look at me.

'Why not? We need this, Duncan.'

'It's not possible.'

'Why not? Don't you want to save these animals?'

'Of course, I do, and I will do anything… but not that.'

'Stop being stubborn and pig-headed. You need to do this.' I was getting exasperated with him.

He looked at me, fury spreading like fire over his face. 'I am not being stubborn or pig-headed, I am being realistic.' He could see I was not ready to give up. 'Do not ask me to do this thing. I cannot do it!' he barked. He looked so angry then that I felt a knot of fear churn in my stomach. I took a step back, turned, and headed back to the stairwell.

'I thought you said you'd do anything to save these beautiful creatures,' I said, unable to keep the steeliness from my voice. I paused at the first step, waiting for his reply.

'I did,' he growled, 'and I meant it.'

'Well, do as I ask,' I said through gritted teeth.

'I already told you that I can't do it!' His voice rose. He was good and angry now, but tried to contain it.

'Why not? Why can't you approach your family? We need their help!' I shouted. 'Jesus! You are so stubborn!'

'I can't do it because I am banished from them, okay?' he yelled back. His sudden outburst startled the creatures, who cried in fright and dived into the water. 'Now look what you made me do!' He glared at me, his eyes daring me to shout at him again, but I did not. The ire that had been growing inside of me suddenly melted away and I felt pity for him.

'What happened?' My voice was calm. Soothing.

'I don't want to talk about it, okay?'

'It might help.'

He stood with his back to me, staring out to where the creatures had taken refuge in the middle of the underground loch. With a deep sigh, he turned around and walked over to where I was waiting for him. He studied me for a moment.

'Alright, I'll tell you all about it, but let's get upstairs first and have some tea.'

He did not speak to me again until the kettle was filled and placed over the fire. Then he busied himself with getting two cups and a teapot ready. As we waited for the kettle to boil, we sat at his table and I waited patiently for him to start. He seemed to have some difficulty in finding the right words and there was genuine pain in his eyes when he eventually looked up and began.

'As you may know, kelpies have a reputation for enticing humans into the water to drown them.'

'Yes, but why would you do that?'

'For sport. Kelpies and humans have never gotten on. Humans used to hunt us or capture us and make us work for them in our horse's form. Trapping and killing the odd traveller was our way of getting back at your race for all the terrible things you did to ours.' He looked ashamed. 'I know it wasn't right, but it was the way it was until my grandfather outlawed the practice many years ago.' He paused. 'When I was a young man, I was sunning myself on the banks of the River Ness one day when a beautiful young human woman happened to stroll by. She was the most exquisite thing I have ever seen, and I asked her to sit with me for a while to talk. Her name was Janey. She had long, black hair and a beautiful smile. I made her promise to meet me again the following day and the next and the next. Soon we were in love.' There was pain and anguish in his voice. I reached over the table and placed my hand over his. He cleared his throat and continued. 'I wanted to marry her—such things are not unheard of between our two species—and I went to my family to tell them. My parents were, naturally, upset that their son wanted to wed a human, they had plans to betroth me to another kelpie maiden, and demanded I bring her to them so that they might see if she was worthy of me or not… which I did. She was nervous, but charming and I thought things were going well.' Here his voice broke, and he paused to compose himself.

'Are you alright?' I asked.

'Yes.' He stood up and went to the kettle, which was beginning to boil. Taking a cloth to protect his hand, he removed it from its hook over the fire and took it to the table. He poured the water into a teapot and returned the kettle to the fireside. 'Anyway, they seemed to like her and, after much persuasion, eventually blessed the marriage. Janey and I planned to wed on Midsummer's Night under the stars. It was to be a traditional kelpie wedding and then we were to do a church wedding the following day. It was all arranged.'

'So, what happened?'

'The day before, Janey came to dinner with my family. Afterwards, I walked her home and left her at her parent's house. She was still alive when I left her. You have to believe that.' He was earnest. 'The next day I found her body in the loch, drowned. Of course, her people blamed me. They said I was a kelpie , and that's what kelpies did. They bandied together and came to my family's home and made all sorts of threats. My father blamed me for bringing all this trouble on them. He didn't believe me when I told him I had not killed her. I loved her. He said Kelpies could never truly love humans. We argued and… well, to appease her family and our clan elders, he banished me.' He poured some tea into my cup and then into his own. He sat down on his chair.

'Did you ever find out how she drowned? She didn't kill herself, did she?'

He looked at me like I was crazy. 'That is not possible. We were happy together.'

'Do you think someone killed her?'

The look he gave me confirmed it.

'But who and why?'

'Those are the same two questions I've been asking myself,'

he said. 'Did her own people do it to stop her marrying a kelpie or was it one of my clan?'

'Could it have been an accident?'

He shook his head. 'I don't think so. She had bruising on her wrists and around her neck like someone had forced her into the water.' He looked at me with those big sad eyes and added: 'I think she was murdered.'

'I'm so sorry, Duncan, I really am.'

'Some folk round here still think I did it and treat me so. Then there are others, like Mrs. Mackintosh at the inn, who have always thought me innocent.... which, of course, I am. Why would I kill Janey? I loved her. I had everything to gain by marrying her. I had nothing to gain through her death.'

'Did you ever try to find out who might have killed her?'

'Yes, but I got nowhere, and it didn't help that I was banished from the clan.'

We slipped into silence for a while, each caught up in our own thoughts. Then he looked at me, worry written all over his face.

'What are we going to do? Dwell seems so determined to get at the creatures. How are we going to stop him?'

'By appealing to your family for help.'

'I can't do that.'

'You should at least try for their sake.'

'Yes, why don't you listen to the little lady?' The voice, sarcastic and sleazy, was oh-so-too-familiar.

# Chapter 8

We looked round to see Dwell and Cassius standing at the doorway of Duncan's home, both holding hunting rifles. Duncan stood up and Dwell immediately trained his weapon on him.

'Stay where you are,' he said. He motioned with the gun that Duncan should put his hands up. Reluctantly, he did. 'I will shoot if you try anything funny.'

'Get out of my home!' Duncan hissed. 'Get out!'

'Not so fast!' Cassius now had his gun trained on the kelpie . 'You stay right where you are. My master has business with Miss Abercrombie.'

Dwell now turned his attention to me and he smiled cruelly. 'So, you thought you could sabotage my plans by damaging our boat, did you?'

I stood up, gave him by best look of defiance, and deigned not to answer.

'Well, your little plan backfired. Even now, I have Warrington securing me a new, bigger boat so we might continue our hunt. We'll be back out on the loch by tomorrow and there's nothing you can do about it.'

'I can tell the local people what you're planning. I can call the local constable to stop you,' I said. I curled my hands into fists in anger.

'You'll do no such thing,' Dwell promised. He examined the tea things on the table and smirked. 'You see, you've become a bit of a liability to me, Miss Abercrombie. You're never there when I need you and you do a poor job when you do turn up…'

I opened my mouth to object, but he talked right over me.

'… So, I need to decide what I'm going to do with you.' He walked over to me and put his hand up to my face. I pulled away, but I still felt his icy fingers stroke my cheek. 'Such a pretty face,' he said. 'Such a shame, really.'

'What do you mean?' The tone of his voice, the look in his eyes, all spoke of danger.

'I mean, I plan to kill both you and your friend over there before I go and kill the creature.'

That did it. Before I could stop him, Duncan had lunged at Cassius and had yanked the hunting rifle from the startled little man's hands. He then spun around and trained the rifle on Dwell. The cryptozoologist was ready for him. He grabbed me around my waist, all the time holding the rifle on Duncan. Then he dragged me further back into the room, towards the tunnel that led down to the underground loch. I felt him lean back, and I knew he was looking down the stairs.

'Cassius, have a look and see where this leads, will you, while I finish talking to our friends here?'

'You'll stay where you are!' Duncan said, pointing the gun at Cassius, but the little man just gave him a haughty laugh.

'When shall we tell him that the rifle isn't loaded, Cassius?' Dwell said. His mouth was close to my ear, and it made me flinch every time he spoke.

Cassius gave Duncan a dirty look as he walked towards the tunnel. 'I think he already knows,' the little man sniggered. He gave me the once over before opening the curtain and disappearing downstairs. My stomach lurched, and I prayed the creatures were out of sight. I silently begged them not to be their usual curious selves and want to inspect the new being in their midst, but I knew all my prayers would not be answered. It would only be a matter of minutes before Cassius would return with the news that there was not only one creature, but a family of four . I waited in trepidation for his footsteps to return to the surface. Dwell seemed oblivious to my fears. Keeping a tight grip on me, he instructed Duncan to put down his weapon and to sit at the table. From where I was being held, I could see Duncan was as anxious for the creatures as I was. He kept glancing towards the doorway, something that was not lost on Dwell.

'You've got something precious down there, haven't you?' He gloated. 'I wonder what it is? What could be hidden down there? Gold? Diamonds? … A monster?'

'Dr . Dwell! Dr . Dwell! Come quickly! You'll never believe this.' Cassius' excited voice rang like a bell from the tunnel.

'I'll be there in just one minute.' He let me go, pushing me towards Duncan. I stumbled and nearly fell, but righted myself. Before I could do anything else, before I could go to my friend, Dwell hit me on the head with the butt of the rifle. I felt a sharp pain and then blacked out. The last thing I remembered was the sound of a gun firing and then nothing.

I awoke sometime later with the mother of all headaches. Groaning, I sat up and opened my eyes.

'What happened?' I said aloud. My voice sounded weak and trembling. I tried to remember, but my head was befuddled and aching. I looked around. I was in Duncan's home. Duncan! I frantically looked around for my friend and saw him lying in a pool of blood on the floor beside the table. Scrambling to my feet, I rushed to him, crying out his name, fearful that he was dead. I knelt down beside him and inspected his deathly white face. It was cold to the touch.

'Duncan! Duncan!' I shouted, desperate for those lovely brown eyes to open and for him to recognise me. 'Wake up!'

He did not move. I inspected his body. Blood stained the front of his white shirt and seeped on to the floor. I gripped the neckline of the shirt and ripped it open to reveal a nasty bullet wound in Duncan's chest. Blood oozed from it and showed no signs of stopping. I placed my head on his chest and listened for a heartbeat. There it was, weak, but there. He was still alive. I sat back and thought frantically as to what I should do.

I looked around, searching for something to stem the blood flow. Seeing nothing useful, I stood up, lifted my skirt and began to tear a strip off my petticoat. With sheer determination and fear I was already too late , I used up all my strength to rip the cotton skirt. I tore off a strip and used it to stem the flow. Placing Duncan's own hand over the rag, I went to his bed and grabbed a pillow and a grey woollen blanket. The pillow I placed under his head and then I covered him with the blanket. What now? I had to get help, but I couldn't move him by myself. He was too heavy. Maybe if I ran to get help…

'Esther .' Duncan's voice was weak, almost a whisper. I rushed to his side.

'Shhhh, don't say too much, you've been shot.' I stroked his cheek, aiming to sooth his worried face.

'The creatures.'

'Never mind them for now, I'll see to them later. We need to get you help.'

'Get me some water,' he said. I nodded and got to my feet. I went to the kitchen table and removed the full water jug. 'No! Not that water,' he croaked. With great effort, with his left hand, he pointed towards the stairs leading down to the underground cave. 'From the loch.' I put the water jug down and fetched a pail which Duncan kept next to the cooker.

'I'll just be a minute,' I promised him. I grabbed a lantern from a hook next to that door and lit it. Giving him one last look, I slipped through the curtains and hurried down the stairs. I did my best to negotiate those stairs properly, but my haste and fear for Duncan's life made me clumsy and I found myself slipping more than once. At last, I reached the bottom and hurried to the water.

There was no sign of the creatures, nor of Dwell or Cassius, but they would have to wait for the moment. I had more pressing matters to attend to. I plunged the bucket into the water and dragged it out, full and dripping with icy loch water. Lugging it up the stairs, I must have spilled a fair amount, but I did not care. Duncan needed this life-saving water, and I was going to make sure he had it. I emerged into his living area moments later to find him slipping into unconsciousness again.

'Duncan! No!' I placed the bucket on the floor beside him and knelt down. I searched for his pulse and could barely feel it. I placed a hand over his mouth, looking for breath. There was none. I listened to his chest for a heartbeat. There was silence. 'No! Duncan, come on! What do you want me to do with this water?' I grabbed him by the shoulders and gently shook him, but he was out of it. I frantically looked around me, desperate to find something to help, and my eyes alighted on the table where the teacups still sat. Scrambling to my feet, I grabbed my cup, emptied the remnants of my tea out of it, and used it to scoop up some water. I took this to Duncan and carefully poured some in his mouth. Much of it slid down either side of his face, but I prayed enough had gone in. Then I took the rag from his wound, dunked it into the water, and bathed his wound. At first, all it did was dissipate the blood, but as I continued dabbing it, something miraculous happened. The wound began to throb and move on its own. Using the cup again, I scooped up some more water and threw it on his chest. It ran down his ribs, taking streaks of blood with it, but some had gone into the bullet hole. Then something odd happened. Something was moving and working its way up to the surface. The bullet hole widened and a blooded bullet worked its way out of Duncan's body. It was long and made of brass, and I plucked it out and set it aside. Then I watched, fascinated, as the large wound in Duncan's chest began to mend itself. Firstly, the interior blood vessels, bone and muscle began to meld together, back to where they should be. Then the skin began to knit closed. Within seconds, the wound had completely closed over. Then the scar disappeared and you would have never known there had been a bullet hole there. I stared at it in horrified fascination. What had just happened? Satisfied I could do no more on that matter, I scooped up some more water with the cup and dribbled it over Duncan's lips. His lips twitched, then a pink tongue appeared, licking the water up. His mouth opened, and he accepted the cup. He drank a little, then he drank some more.

'Take your time,' I murmured to him as he pulled himself up on to his elbows and began to drink deeply from the cup. 'I don't want you drowning.' That remark made him pause, open his eyes, and give me a rueful smile.

'There's no danger of that,' he said. 'I'm a kelpie , remember?'

'How are you feeling?'

'A lot better,' he said, placing a hand on my arm, 'thanks to you.'

Then it happened. We shared a moment. Yes, that's exactly what it was. A moment. A magical interlude of time where everything else fades into the background and there was only him and me. I had never experienced the like before. It was wonderful. I truly felt a deep connection with him at that point. Did he feel the same about me? Without drawing his eyes from mine, Duncan carefully sat up, reached out and pulled me towards him. Gazing intently at me, he drew me closer and gently kissed me on the lips. I must have gasped, for he paused and looked at me searchingly. I smiled. He smiled, and he kissed me again. It took my breath away; my heart raced with joy, my body trembled with excitement and I could hardly believe the pleasure that such a small thing brought to my body and soul.

'Thank you for saving me,' he whispered.

'I did nothing... really...' I began.

'You did everything,' he said. He took a breath and pulled away, a worried look on his face. The mood darkened. 'The creatures? Did you see them when you went to collect the water? Are they safe?'

'I didn't see them. I don't know where they are.'

He nodded. 'Can you help me to get up? I'm still feeling a little unsteady?' He offered me his arm, and I took it. I heaved him to his feet and stood close by while he inspected the bullet hole site. There was barely a mark there. 'That gun packed a punch! Still, it takes a lot to kill a kelpie !' he joked.

'You nearly died!' I suddenly felt very shaky and close to tears. The enormity of the ordeal suddenly hit me. I had come so close to losing the only man I loved.

'But I didn't.' He took a couple of shaky steps before pausing.

'Where are you going? You need to rest.'

'I need to find the creatures. I need to know that they are safe.' He walked towards the doorway leading down into the loch.

'Well, I'm coming with you.'

In the cavern, Duncan stood at the water's edge and called and called for the creatures. It was a loud, guttural cry rather like that of a seabird except lower in tone. After every call, he paused, waiting to hear a response or to see those familiar grey bodies emerge from the water, but no creature came.

'Where are they?' he said desperately. I touched his arm.

'I don't know.'

'He's taken them, hasn't he? He's got them in that barn and he's cutting into them even now.'

'We don't know that.' The words came out, but I didn't believe them myself. Duncan didn't either, going by the look he gave me.

'Now, what do we do? I can't compete against hunting rifles. There's only so many bullets a kelpie can take.'

'Now we have to enlist some help,' I said. Before he could protest, I added: 'We have no choice, Duncan. I'm sure they will be just as concerned as we are about the creatures' safety. It's in their interests as well as ours to get those beasts back.'

He looked at me, and there was an almost imperceptible nod of his head. 'Alright, but I'm going alone. It's too dangerous.'

'No,' I replied. 'I'm coming with you… and before you say anything, I'm in this with you. You can't do this by yourself and I want to help.'

He took my hand and gave it a squeeze. 'Alright, but you

have to do everything I say when I say it. My family doesn't like humans and it could be dangerous. Agreed?'

'Agreed.'

# Chapter 9

Duncan thought it would be quicker to reach the River Ness and the firth by boat. The roads north to Inverness were not good in those days, so it seemed like a good plan. The only problem was finding one. It was late afternoon by the time we snuck back to the inn. Keeping to the bushes and trees, we took up position close to the barn and watched and waited. Although the puffer was still docked at the jetty, there was no sign of Dwell, Warrington or of Cassius. I snuck up to the barn window and got Duncan to give me a leg up so that I might see inside. Wiping away years of dirt from the glass pane, I created a hole big enough to see. The barn was empty save for a few abandoned pieces of equipment and the automatons standing together in a row like soldiers on parade. The knives were gone, along with the metal netting. The box of explosives remained. There were no signs of the creatures. Any creatures. Unsure of what was happening, I climbed back down and told Duncan of my findings.

'Where would they have taken them?' he asked as I sorted my skirts.

'I don't know.' I thought for a moment. 'Wait here. I think I know someone who might.'

I crept up to the inn and slipped through the kitchen door at the back of the building. I found Mrs. Mackintosh at the stove, stirring a large black cauldron of soup. She started when she saw me.

'Oooh! You gave me a right fright there,' she said.

'Sorry, Mrs. Mackintosh, I didn't mean to.'

'Do you want some soup? It's lentil.' She gave the delicious smelling soup a stir.

'No, thank you. I just need to find out where Dr. Dwell has gone.'

'Dr. Dwell? He and his companions checked out two hours ago. That Mr. Warrington had secured them another boat; it came down the Ness into the loch about three hours ago and picked them up close to the jetty. I think they're heading for Inverness. Dr Dwell mentioned he had further studies to do there.'

'Did you see them leave? Did they have anything with them?'

'Like what?'

'The creatures. They're missing.'

She looked alarmed. 'I didn't go out. It was Adam that saw them and he never mentioned any creatures.'

I thought for a moment. 'Is there anyone here who can take us up to Inverness? We need to follow them, make sure the creatures aren't with them.'

'No, sorry, lass, we've only got rowing boats for fishing round here. You need something with a bit more power to get you up the River Ness. Why don't you see if Captain Buchan will take you? One of his men told me they thought they had located the part they needed. They got it from someone in Drumnadrochit.'

I thanked her and went to look for her son. Adam was in the bar clearing glasses and tankards from the tables when I approached. I asked him about the boat Dwell had chartered and he gave me a fairly good description, even remembering its name. It was a schooner called The Lady Georgina.

I returned to Duncan waiting outside and told him what I'd learned. He was not keen ongoing on the puffer again, especially as it had been he who had sabotaged it, but we could see no other option. He wasn't yet strong enough to follow Dwell's new boat himself, so the puffer it was.

'I know how we can get round this,' I said.

It took Duncan five minutes to locate the missing puffer part and pull it out of the loch. Then we went to Captain Buchan and begged for his assistance. As Duncan handed him the dripping part, we told him what we knew of Dwell and his intentions; we explained that the creatures were missing, and that we were worried he had them. He seemed nonplussed, and still angry.

'Why should I do anything for you two? You sabotaged my boat!' he yelled, waving the engine part in our faces. 'If Blair hadn't managed to get me a spare part, we wouldna have been able to go anywhere.'

'I'm sorry,' Duncan replied.

'We'll pay you for the part,' I added. 'Please Captain Buchan, please.'

He shook his head, but only began to show interest when I offered to pay for over the odds for our fare. I had a little money about my person, wages Dwell had given to me before, and promised him the lot.

'Alright,' he said. 'Give us ten minutes to fit this again and then we'll be off.'

Within half an hour, the puffer was gently making its way

to the northernmost end of Loch Ness and into the much smaller Loch Dochfour. From there we continued north until we reached the beginning of the Caledonian Canal, which runs alongside the River Ness. Built nearly one hundred years before, the canal was still a busy waterway and made our trip to Inverness far faster and easier. Carefully negotiating its way down the canal, the little boat took us up to the Moray Firth, the wide estuary where the river met the sea, and then on to the northern town of Inverness. As Buchan and his crew manoeuvred the little boat into the northernmost point of the River Ness and headed south again, I got my first glimpse of the town. It was a good size town with a harbour busy with dock workers loading and unloading goods boats. Further on, I could see the outlines of tall church steeples and Inverness Castle dominating the skyline. But we weren't there to visit and enjoy, we were there to find Dwell.

As the puffer docked, I desperately looked around for any large vessel that could have been Dwell's boat, but couldn't see anything that fit the bill. There were several fishing boats, a barge weighed down with coal and two sloops being packed with what looked like bales of sheep's wool. But no schooner. Where could they be? Surely, they hadn't already put out to sea? Duncan must have been thinking the same thing, for his face was frantic with searching and there was fear in his eyes. I suggested we disembark and ask around to see if anyone had seen it. I approached an older sailor first. He was a small man with a weather-beaten face who smoked a long clay pipe. He sucked on it thoughtfully when I asked him if he had seen the The Lady Georgina.

'I might have done,' he said. 'What's in it for me?' He winked.

'What do you mean?' I was still a young woman then and

while I thought he meant something salacious; I couldn't be sure. Surely, he didn't mean for me to…? I was a decent woman. I would never…

'Coins,' he replied, much to my relief. He held out a bony, calloused hand. It was ingrained with dirt and engine grease.

'Well, how do I know that the information you give me is what I'm looking for?' In my gut, I knew I couldn't trust this man.

He leered at me. 'You don't.' He sucked on his pipe and watched me closely. Then he said: 'It's coins or nothing.'

I did not know what to do at that point, for I had no money with me. I had given it all to Captain Buchan. I felt tears well in my eyes and suddenly felt very tired. The stress of it all was finally taking its toll.

'I have no money,' I admitted.

'Well, then, no information,' he said. Then he cocked his head to one side and added: 'You're not a bad-looking woman. Maybe we could come to some sort of arrangement.' He got to his feet and stood beside me, looking me over like I was a prize mare.

'What sort of arrangement?' I felt extremely uncomfortable.

'Well, maybe you could make a fella happy, if you catch my drift?' He leered at me and licked his lips. I shuddered.

'How dare you!' I said, my voice small. 'How dare you!' I looked him right in the eye and said it louder. 'If you think that I would…!'

'What's going on?' Duncan was at my side, looking concerned.

Not wishing to cause a scene, people were already looking at us, I lied. 'Nothing, this man has no information about The Lady Georgina.'

'Are you alright?'

'Yes, fine. Let's go.'

Duncan eyed the sailor suspiciously, before offering me his arm. He steered me in the direction of the puffer and told me he had good news.

'I spoke to the harbour master. He said The Lady Georgina docked here briefly to take on supplies. He said the captain informed him he was making for Edinburgh and was boasting that Dwell had offered him a huge sum to get there quickly. He said they caused quite a stir in the town because they had a large cage on board that was covered up by tarps, but that something was crying out behind it.'

'So, he does have the creatures!' It was such a relief to know they were still alive. 'How are we going to get to Edinburgh?' I wanted to know. 'Plus, we've still got to speak to your family. We're never going to get there in  time.' I could feel the panic rise in my chest.

'We take it one step at a time,' he said, patting my hand. 'My family live a little way out of town. I will speak to Captain Buchan and see if he can take us to Edinburgh. The puffer isn't as fast as the ship Dwell is on, but it is seaworthy and will get us to the city safely.' He let go of my arm. 'Wait here, I'll just be a minute.'

As I waited on the dock, I tried my best to curb the anxiety that had been growing in me since I learned that Dwell had stolen the creatures. They were beautiful, rare creatures, and I knew he would kill them soon. I just hoped we could get there in time. I stood watching the dock workers, sailors and locals mill about on the stone pier and marvelled at how calm and collected they all were. They were going about their day as if nothing bad was happening and I had to fight the anger rising in my core.

How could they all be so calm when even now Dwell could be murdering those wonderful creatures? Of course, those feelings were unreasonable. How could they be expected to know? But the fear that gripped my insides just would not dispel and made me jumpy and upset.

From where I was standing, I could see Duncan was having an animated conversation with Buchan. He glanced over at me, his eyes telling me that things were taking a bad turn. Then he nodded and returned to my side.

'He wants payment,' he said gruffly. 'I have no money.' He looked at me and I shook my head. 'Damn it! He says he's going nowhere unless we pay up front for the trip to Edinburgh.'

My heart sank at that moment. 'What are we going to do?' I placed my hand on his arm. He looked so worried.

'I'm going to have to ask my family for money.' He did not look happy at the prospect, but there was nothing else he could do. If we had any hope of saving the creatures, he had to approach the family. I gave his arm a squeeze.

'It's going to be fine, Duncan. We're going to save them.'

The look he gave me, the worry and sorrow in those beautiful eyes, would have broken any heart. He took in a deep breath. Then he looked at me, determination returning to his face. He cleared his throat. 'Well, we're not going to save them standing around here,' he said. 'Come on, let's go and get it over with.'

'What about Captain Buchan?' I didn't want the puffer leaving without us.

'I've told him I have the money. He's going to take on some more coal and some other things he needs. He says he'll wait for us.'

The journey to Duncan's family took us well out of Inverness itself. We headed east and walked for more than an hour, barely talking as my companion brooded on his task ahead. Before we set off, he had confessed he was nervous about seeing his family again and those nerves grew the closer we got to the area where they lived. Five miles east of Inverness, near the village of Culloden and the famous battlefield, we left the dirt track that was the road and headed across rough ground towards the sea. Tripping and staggering over the pitted ground, I did my best to keep up as Duncan strode towards a tumbledown shack on the edge of the beach. He slowed down on the approach, allowing me to join him.

'Is this it?' I asked, somewhat breathlessly. Ladies' boots were definitely not made for walking over the grassy dunes at the beach. I glanced down at my skirts and sighed. They were covered in grass seed and sand. I must have looked a fright. This was no way to meet Duncan's family. I quickly brushed some of it off, hoping they would not notice how dishevelled I was or see the torn parts of my underskirts.

He looked at me, saw what I was doing, and frowned. 'Yes, this is the entrance.' He walked to the small wooden door and knocked. From inside, we heard someone muttering. There were the sounds of movement and then an old man opened the door.

'What do you want?' he barked, peering out at us through half-rimmed spectacles. He was a small man, bent double with age and wrinkled. He wore moleskin trousers, a striped shirt, and a waistcoat with a gold watch chain. His bald head was bare, but he sported an impressive set of mutton chops on his cheeks. He leaned on a wooden walking stick.

'Marcus?' Duncan looked for recognition in the old man's eyes.

Marcus stepped forward and studied Duncan closely. He looked him over from top to bottom. 'Is it really you?'

112

'Yes, it's me.'

'Do they know you're here?'

'No.'

'Hmmph.' He stepped back and then grinned. 'Welcome back, Your Highness, it's been too long.'

He opened his arms, and Duncan stepped forward for a warm hug. I looked at Duncan in astonishment. Your Highness? Was Duncan royalty?

# Chapter 10

'It's good to see you, Marcus,' Duncan said as he straightened up.

'So, are you here to make amends? You've been missed, you know.'

'I'm here on a mission of mercy,' he said. 'I don't have time to go into it right now, but I need to speak with my father.'

'And who's your fair companion?' Marcus wanted to know. He was now looking at me, his beady little eyes boring through me. 'Another human? Is that wise Duncan? You know what happened last time.'

Duncan looked at me and then looked back at Marcus. 'She will be fine with me. I will protect her,' he said. 'Now, are you going to let us by or not? We're in a hurry.'

The old man smiled, nodded, and then turned to walk back inside. 'Well, you must know what you're doing. Come on then, follow me. Not that I need to show you the way!'

'Are you sure I should be coming with you?' I whispered to Duncan as we followed Marcus into the shack.

He gave my hand a squeeze. 'You're safe so long as you're with me.'

Marcus led us through the sparsely furnished building to a small stone-built doorway at the rear. It had an ornately carved wooden door that looked too heavy for the man to open. However, with the ease of someone half his age, he yanked it open and stood there as first Duncan and then I walked through.

'Is he a kelpie like you?' I asked as I followed Duncan down a stone corridor. It had been built with large boulders and gently sloped downwards. It was lit with burning torches in metal sconces attached to the walls at regular intervals.

'Who Marcus? No. He's human. He and his family have been guarding the entranceway to our kingdom for centuries.

'Is that where he lives? In that shack?'

He turned to face me, a grin playing about his lips. 'Do you think we would allow a loyal servant to live in such a lowly place? No, he has a comfortable cottage further along the beach where he lives with his wife. He and his sons and daughters take turns in guarding the entranceway. We were just lucky he was on duty just now.'

'Why? Would his sons and daughters not have let us in?' My head was full of imagined fierce adult children shaking sticks at us whilst denying us entry.

'They would have, but we would have been kept at the door for a time as they questioned us about our relationship,' he replied. 'The girls, especially, were always asking me about my love life.'

The tunnel took us down into the earth some more and finally came to a set of stairs leading even further down. Duncan offered me his hand and helped me down the steep stone stairwell. There must have been about fifty steps to negotiate in the semi-darkness, no mean feat for someone in long skirts, but we managed it and came to a wide archway that opened out into a massive cavern. Illuminated using a complicated combination of oil lanterns and mirrors, the effect was to provide a feeling almost like daylight. I blinked as my eyes grew accustomed to this new light.

'Welcome to Caomhain, my hometown,' Duncan said. He took my hand and gave it a squeeze. He must have sensed my nervousness.

I looked around me and was delighted to see a pretty little place consisting of neat stone cottages with slate roofs. A single street split the town and led to a larger building at the end. Each cottage had its own yard at the rear and, on one side of the street, each yard opened up onto  an underground lake in which a number of children and adults were bathing. There were also a number of people milling about on the street, going about their business. They did not notice us at first, but as Duncan and I walked hand-in-hand into the town, I could feel their curious gazes on us. No-one spoke to us as we made our way towards the larger house, but I could hear them muttering amongst themselves.

'Is that him? No, it can't be. Is it him? I think it is!'

Duncan ignored them all, striding confidently towards the house he called the palace.

'It's not as grand as some of your human palaces,' he said as we approached the entranceway, 'but it's a palace none-the-less.'

It was not grand at all. It resembled the cottages in as much as it was built from boulders, but it was about five times larger and had actual glass at the many windows. The houses owned by the townspeople, Duncan explained, only had shutters at theirs.

'Being underground, the temperature remains the same all year round,' he explained, 'so we don't need glass to keep the heat in. My great-grandfather had it installed because he liked it.'

'This is your family's home?' I asked.

'Yes.' He approached the large door and used the horse-head brass door knocker to knock. 'It's a bit grander inside.'

'I think it's lovely,' I said, and I meant it. There was a charm about the place. It reminded me of some of the old farmhouses I was used to growing up in Ayrshire.

There were the sounds of footsteps coming towards us and we braced ourselves as the door opened to reveal a young man dressed in a dark blue tunic and trousers. He held a book in his hand and looked at us quizzically.

'May I help you?'

'I'm here to speak with the King,' Duncan replied.

'State your business.' The man was staring at me like I'd grown horns.

'It's none of yours,' Duncan snapped. 'Just let me in. I need to speak with my father.'

The young man looked at Duncan in surprise and it was only then that recognition swept over his face. 'Prince Duncan? Is that really you?'

'Yes, it is, Harald,' Duncan replied. 'Hurry, I have urgent business.'

Harald snapped to attention. He saluted his sovereign prince. 'Yes, yes, of course.' He stood back and opened the door wider to allow us entry. 'I'm sorry I didn't recognise Your Highness,' the poor man stuttered. 'It's been a long time and…'

Duncan patted him on the shoulder. 'It's alright, Harald. I'm sorry I was so rude. Now, where is the King?'

'I believe His Majesty is in his laboratory,' Harald replied, frowning as I walked by. 'Is she a human? We don't allow humans here; you know the rules.'

Duncan turned around and gave the young man a hard stare,

causing Harald to gulp. 'She's with me,' he growled. 'Come on, Esther . This way.'

I looked in awe at the interior of the house. There was a large reception hallway with beautifully carved wall panelling depicting the fruits of the sea: fish and seaweed and all sorts of creatures. Three large oil paintings, two of women and one man, dominated the walls. There was a large gold and crystal chandelier hanging from the ceiling and the whole room was carpeted with a deep blue woollen carpet. Pressed against the walls were fine Chippendale chairs and tables, on which stood candelabras and other nick-nacks. Duncan led me through a door to the left into a narrow corridor lined either side by family portraits dating back to medieval  times. The corridor ended at a large wooden door, where Duncan paused. He let go of my hand and knocked. Boom, boom, boom.

'Come in.' The voice, a deep baritone, rang out from within.

Duncan pushed open the door to reveal a fully equipped laboratory and a large man with wavy white jaw-length hair standing at a table wearing an artist's smock and goggles. He removed the goggles immediately and seemed stunned to see who it was.

'Is it really you?' He said, astonished.

'Hello Dad,' Duncan said. He was nervous and seemed to be a shadow of himself.

His father walked around the table, arms out, and pulled his son into his arms. Giving him a bear hug, he said: 'I never thought I'd see you again. After you left, we looked everywhere for you, but we could find no trace. Where have you been, son?' He let his son go and held him by his hands. There were tears in his eyes.

It was Duncan's turn to look confused. 'I've been living at Loch Ness, in the old holiday home.'

'What do you mean? I sent Arthur to investigate Loch Ness, and he said you weren't there, that no one had seen you. He said the home was empty. Do you mean to tell me you've been there the entire time?'

'I've not seen Arthur, not since I left…' Duncan said. 'He never came to the cave.'

The King's eyes narrowed, and he let Duncan go. 'I will be speaking to Arthur when he gets back,' he said in a low tone. Then his eyes swivelled to me and I wished I was invisible. He gave me such a piercing look; it was all I could do to stand there and not run for my life. 'Who is this?' His voice was flat.

'This is Esther.' Duncan walked to my side and put his arm around my shoulder. 'She is my… friend.'

Friend? Is that all I am to you? I wondered as disappointment pierced my gut.

'She's been helping me,' Duncan continued.

'You know the rules about bringing humans to Caomhaim,' the King said. There was a sadness in his voice. 'You know what happened last time?'

'I know, but this is exceptional circumstances,' Duncan said. 'Please, Father. She needs to be here.'

The King looked me over once more and then his stern face softened. 'Alright, well, you'd better introduce us then.'

Looking pleased, Duncan said: 'Father, may I introduce you to Miss Esther Abercrombie of Ayrshire?' Then he turned to me. 'Esther, may I introduce you to my father, King Fergus the White, of Caomhaim.'

I dropped to a curtsey and bowed my head. 'Your Majesty,' I said. The older man seemed pleased.

'Well, at least she has manners,' he said. Then he focussed back on Duncan. 'So, what's so urgent you break our rules for?'

'It's about the creatures of Loch Ness,' Duncan began. And then he proceeded to tell his father all about Dwell and his plans for the monsters. He told him about my involvement in it all, how I had saved his life not once but twice, and where we believed Dwell was taking them now. 'We need your help, Father ,' he concluded. 'We need some men and some… money.'

His father nodded sagely, listening to every word before walking away from us, evidently deep in thought. After a few minutes, he turned back again.

'I can give you some money,' he said, 'but giving you men might be difficult. Many of them are out at sea on a hunting trip. I only have a handful left to guard this place.'

'What about Sophie and her women?' Duncan wanted to know. I looked at him wondering who Sophie was, but he didn't appear to notice.

'I doubt she has time. She's in the middle of wedding preparations,' the King said. He rubbed his chin. 'She's marrying Angus, you know Angus? Perry's youngest boy!'

Duncan nodded.

'Well, I suppose there would be no harm in asking her,' the King went on. 'I'm sure she'll help if she can.'

'Thanks Dad ,' Duncan said. He offered his father his hand. The King took his hand in both of his and shook it warmly. Then he gave his son a look of affection and pulled him in for a bear hug. Several moments went by as both men hugged each other before the King finally released Duncan.

'Now, before you go off looking for Sophie, you'll be wanting something to eat. Your mother will be furious if I don't at least feed you.' The King wiped his eyes. The emotion of seeing his son again seemed to have really affected him.

'Where is Mum ?'

'In the library, I believe,' the older man replied. 'She's aye got her nose stuck in a book.' He turned to me. 'Well, Esther , will you join me for some food? I believe there's crab meat on the menu today.'

'That would be delightful, Your Majesty, but I don't think Duncan and I have the time to spare,' I said, looking at my kelpie love. 'We need to get after Dwell and stop him before he kills the creatures.'

'Ah, yes, yes, of course,' the King said regretfully. 'Well, I'll just get the kitchen to make you up a basket so you can take some with you.' He walked towards the door. 'Come on, walk me out.'

He offered me his arm, and I took it, and together we walked through the door. As he led me along the corridor, he thanked me profusely for saving his son's life.

'It was the least I could do, Your Majesty.' I said. 'I couldn't leave him to die.'

'Never-the-less you have my undying gratitude,' the King replied.

We reached the entrance hall and paused underneath the enormous chandelier. The King patted my arm.

'This is where I must leave you, my dear.' He released me and turned to Duncan. 'I am so glad you have returned, my son. You've made an old man very happy.'

There were tears in Duncan's eyes. 'I'm glad I've come back. I'm sorry I stayed away for so long.'

'That's what I don't understand, Son ,' the King said. 'What made you leave in the first place?'

Duncan looked confused. 'You banished me. I was told that if I didn't leave there and then for the murder of Janey, I would be executed. I was given some money and made to go.'

It was Fergus's turn to look puzzled. 'I never gave that order. Janey's death was deemed an accident. You were never accused of her murder.'

'But…!'

The palace door burst open. 'Hallo cousin!' A tall, thin man with a face like a weasel entered the palace, a broad grin on his face. 'So, the rumours are true. You are back!' He grabbed Duncan and gave him a bear hug.

'Arthur, how are you?' Duncan said coldly. He carefully extricating himself from his cousin's grip.

'All the better for seeing you,' Arthur replied. There was a smile on his face, but I noticed it didn't touch his pale grey eyes. There was something off about Arthur.

'Are you?' Duncan didn't sound convinced.

'Of course! We've all missed you very much!'

'Then why did you tell me the King and his ministers had accused me of murdering Janey and had banished me from the kingdom, on pain of death should I ever return?' Duncan's hands were on his hips and he was looking intently at his squirming cousin.

'I never said that!' Arthur retorted. 'Why would I say that? It's ridiculous.'

'On the night I left, you came to me and urged me to flee. You said my life was in danger, that I would be executed if I didn't leave there and then.'

Arthur pursed his lips and shook his head. 'I don't know where you got that fairy tale from, Duncan, but I never said those things.' He tried to return Duncan's stare, but could not meet his eyes, a sure sign he was telling lies. Duncan must have thought so too, for he suddenly strode towards Arthur, grabbed him by the throat and pulled him up off his feet. Arthur squeaked in fright.

'You're lying!' Duncan rasped.

I ran to Duncan's side and tried to reason with him. We did not have time for this, not now. The creatures could be, even at this very moment, being cut up in the name of science.

'Duncan! Let him go! Let him go, Duncan!' I urged. Arthur gave me the creeps and I could understand Duncan's anger, but we had an urgent matter to attend to. His cousin could wait. 'We can't do anything about this today. We need to get back to the boat. Duncan! Are you listening?'

'Yes, listen to the human, Duncan,' Arthur sneered. 'We know you're good at listening to them.' Duncan must have squeezed harder, for Arthur began to choke and his eyes bulged.

'Duncan, let him go!' I yelled.

Duncan glanced at me, took a deep, angry breath and then slowly lowered the whimpering Arthur to the ground. 'I'll deal with you later,' he growled before turning to me. I took his hand and gave it a reassuring squeeze. I looked up and saw Arthur looking at me with interest. It made me extremely uncomfortable. The King broke the atmosphere.

'Arthur, please remove yourself from this palace. I will speak to you about this incident later.' To Duncan, he added: 'Go and speak to your mother in the library. Tell her to give you some money. I will join you shortly after I've sorted out your basket.'

'Thank you, Father,' Duncan said. His voice was quieter, but still brooding.

Arthur left the entrance hall in a hurry, and the king disappeared through another door. Gripping my hand, Duncan led me through yet another door into a large and beautifully decorated library. There were floor-to-ceiling wooden bookcases on three walls and a large window with a view of the town on the other. Comfortable leather sofas were dotted around the room and an impressive oak desk was positioned at one end of the room. It was at this desk sat a glamorous older woman in a fashionable dress. She looked up as we entered and smiled.

'Duncan?' She stood up and rushed to be at her son's side. 'It really is you! I've missed you, darling.' She had a faint French accent. You get kelpies in France? I wondered.

'Mother.' He engulfed her in a hug and suffered her many, many kisses on his cheeks. When she finally settled down, he let her go, and she stood there beaming at him.

'I cannot believe you have returned to us. I am so 'appy,' she cooed.

'We're only here for a brief time,' he said. Then, seeing her face fall, added: 'But I will come again soon, I promise.'

'Well, you must eat something, you've grown so thin...' She felt his bicep and tutted. There was nothing thin about Duncan. He was pure muscle, but only a mother could not see that.

'Mum! Please! I don't have time.' He then quickly introduced me and explained what we were doing there.

'Yes, of course, you must have money,' she said after hearing about the creatures' dire circumstances.

'I thought about asking Sophie and some of her friends to come and help us,' he said, looking at her for approval.

She nodded enthusiastically. 'I can think of no better people to ask,' she replied. She went behind the desk again, opened the drawer, and took out a large metal key. Then she went to a bookcase, pulled a book and the bookcase swung open like a door. There was a tiny room behind it housing a large metal safe. Using the key, she opened the safe and withdrew a bundle of paper money. Closing and locking the safe again, she returned to the room and handed it to Duncan. 'Is this enough?'

Enough? There was at least four hundred pounds there. A fortune in 1898. Duncan didn't seem fazed. He just smiled and nodded. He folded the money carefully and stuffed it in a trouser pocket.

'Thank you,' he said.

His mother gave him a heartfelt hug and bade him farewell. 'You'll find Sophie down by the water.'

Duncan's cousin Sophie was a tall, willowy woman a full head taller than myself. Beautiful, graceful and beguiling, she was everything I was not, and I felt somewhat unattractive beside her. Dressed in a long dark blue velvet gown edged with lace, a silver brooch in the shape of a fern on her breast and a Claymore sword in a sheath at her side, she was standing by a wooden bench shouting encouragement to a group of other women in the water. She had long, dark hair piled high on her head with tendrils framing her beautiful face. She turned around as we approached and looked surprised. A smile broke over her face when she recognised her cousin and she threw herself at him.

'Duncan! You're back! Where have you been?' She cried, giving him a bear hug. 'We've been so worried.'

'I know, I know. I'll explain it all later,' he said. 'But for now, I need your help, Sophie, and I need it fast.'

She let go of him and gave him a puzzled look. 'You sound serious.'

'It is serious.'

Then she noticed me. 'Who's this? Oh, don't tell me you've gone and fallen for a human woman again, Duncan! I thought you would know better! Especially after the last time.'

Putting his hands up to placate her. 'It's not like that!' he said
hastily. 'Esther and I are just friends.' There he goes again, I
thought. We're just friends. I inwardly winced, surprised by how
much his words hurt me. In my head I knew he had to tell his
family these things, but in my heart I was devastated. Is that all
I am to you, I thought, a friend? I didn't have time to mull over
it. Sophie was looking at me with her startling green eyes. She
did not smile.

Then she focussed on Duncan. 'That's good,' she said, patting him on the chest. 'Now, what's so urgent?'

While Duncan told our story, I found my mind drifting away
from them. It suddenly struck me that here I was, a mere human
woman from Ayrshire, who had found herself in an extraordinary situation. I was standing in an unknown kelpie town, with
two kelpies , one of whom was definitely royal, and no-one back
home knew about it. Would they even believe me if I told them?

'Esther !' I suddenly realised Duncan was calling to me.

'Sorry, what?'

'You were miles away. Sophie has agreed to come with us,
but is unable to take any of her battalion. They have to remain
here to guard Caomhain.'

'Battalion?'

'Didn't I say? Sophie is a General in the Caomhain army.'

'You have an army?' I couldn't keep the astonishment out
of my voice. How many other things did I not know about my
home country? And how did they keep all this a secret?

'It's just a small army,' Sophie explained. 'Just in case... Well,
you know.'

'No, sorry, I don't...'

'Well, humans aren't known for being kind to other creatures,' Sophie said. 'We have our army in case of invasion.' Then

something must have occurred to her for she turned to Duncan and said: 'She is alright, isn't she? She won't go and tell on us?'

Duncan looked at me, fondness in his eyes. 'I trust her with my life, Sophie. She'll not give away our secret.'

'I am standing right here, you know,' I grumbled. 'I can answer for myself.'

'Yes, but you are human and, well, many of your people can be duplicitous,' Sophie replied.

I did not know how to answer that, for she was right, but she still shouldn't be standing there insulting my people. I opened my mouth to retort, but was prevented from doing so by a stern look from Duncan.

'We need to get going, Sophie,' he said. 'We need to leave as soon as possible. How quickly can you gather your things?'

'A few minutes.'

# Chapter 11

Twenty minutes later, armed with several baskets of food and wine for the journey courtesy of the King , and a trunk full of travel clothing from the Queen , Duncan and I stood at the front door of the palace waiting for Sophie. She arrived a few minutes later, still armed with her sword, followed by a young man carrying an assortment of weapons in his arms.

'She can't show up in Edinburgh bearing those. She'll be arrested,' I whispered to Duncan.

'Sophie, I'm sorry, you'll need to leave the weapons.'

His cousin frowned. 'But we'll need them when we take on this doctor  human.' She held up her sword and brandished it. 'He's going to be sorry he ever took our creatures.'

'Sophie, you can't!' I said. She scowled and looked at Duncan.

'Who is she to tell me what to do?'

'She's right, Sophie. You must leave them here.'

She pursed her lips. 'Can I at least take some knives? My Sgian Dhus? My dirk?'

'Alright, you can take them…'

Sophie grinned.

'…provided you conceal them about your person,' Duncan said.

'No problem.' She took the sgian dhus from the young man, hitched up her skirts, and stuck one down each garter. They were small single-edged knives that, while normally used for domestic purposes, could also act as weapons. Then she grabbed the dirk, a long-bladed dagger, and carefully put it down her bodice.

'What about these, my lady?' The man held up two tiny knives. 'Your muttacashlass.'

'Oh yes!' She took them and carefully concealed them in her hair, leaving only the hilts in view, looking very much like hair combs. She turned to Duncan again. 'I'm ready.'

'The sword, Sophie.'

She sighed, unbuckled her sword sheath and handed it and the sword to her man. 'Take this home, will you, Aonghas?'

'Yes, my lady.' Aonghas bowed and left, carrying the sword carefully before him. Sophie looked at her cousin.

'Alright?'

'Yes.' He smiled. 'Okay, now we are all here, we need to work out how to get all these things to the boat. I have the money to pay Captain Buchan, so hopefully we could be in Edinburgh some time tomorrow. If I take the clothes chest, do you ladies think you can manage the baskets?'

Just as we were picking up the baskets, the palace doors opened and the King and Queen exited. They both approached Duncan, arms out to give him a hug.

'We couldn't let you leave again without saying goodbye,' his mother said. She kissed him on both cheeks. 'Promise me that once this is over, you will come back?' There were tears in her eyes.

'I will.'

'And be careful.'

He turned to the King . They hugged again. 'Father,' Duncan said. Did his voice just crack with emotion?

'Son.' The older man shook his son's hand. 'Take care of yourself and the women. Get those creatures back where they belong. I know you can do it.'

'I'll die trying.'

'Farewell my son!' The King turned to myself and Sophie. 'Take care of him and bring him back to us,' he said to Sophie. He spoke to me. 'And you make sure he comes home in one piece, too, Miss Abercrombie.'

'I will, sir.' I said with a curtsey.

'Well,' the King began, 'we will bid you fair journey and safe travels. Farewell. Farewell.'

The King and Queen stood on the steps of the palace and watched us as we walked down the main street of Caomhain. When we reached the end of the road, Duncan turned and waved a final goodbye to his parents before leading us up into the tunnel and out onto the beach once more.

Marcus was waiting at the exit as we emerged into the weak sunshine of the afternoon.

'It was nice to see you again, Your Highness,' he said as he gave Duncan a low bow.

'Marcus, there's no need for that. Come on, you've known me since I was a child. No bowing, please.'

The old man straightened up. Duncan put out his hand and shook Marcus' hand vigorously. 'I'll see you again soon, Marcus.'

'I hope so, Your Highness.'

It was late afternoon when the three of us arrived in Inverness. Sophie, unused to being around so many humans, was jumpy, but Duncan soon soothed her ragged nerves by promising her some fine Caomhain wine once on board the puffer. His father had had his kitchen staff pack three bottles of it.

Captain Buchan was not happy to see so many people board his boat. There was barely room for the crew, let alone yet another person. And a woman to boot! But he was soon placated when Duncan slipped him fifty pounds in bank notes.

'That should cover everything, Captain,' Duncan said. He turned to Sophie and me. 'Come on, let's get on board.'

The Captain and his crew watched intently as we boarded the boat carrying our baskets of food and the trunk. Sophie ignored them as we took our places on the bow until the engineer Blair stretched out his hand to touch the basket Sophie was carrying. She hissed loudly at him, showing off a set of fine white teeth and causing the little man to back off and disappear down into the puffer's engine room. Captain Buchan laughed loudly and took his place in the wheelhouse. As Duncan and I settled ourselves on deck, the other two crew members weighed anchor and the little boat chugged out of port.

We were nearly a day behind The Lady Georgina and I could feel anxiety build in the pit of my stomach as I thought about what might have already happened to the creatures. It was already late in the afternoon and we could only travel as long as the light allowed us. Thanks to it being the middle of summer, that meant at least until 10pm when Captain Buchan told us we would definitely have to dock at a port for the night.

'Is there no way we can travel at night?' Duncan asked.

'And risk running aground? Definitely not, but I promise you we will be off at first light.' Buchan said. 'Don't worry, I'll get you there as soon as I can.'

And so, the little puffer steamed along at the sedate speed

of five knots per hour as we, the passengers, sat on deck enjoying the summer sun and the spray of the ocean on our faces. Several hours later, with the dark threatening us on the horizon, Captain Buchan took his small ship into the sheltered harbour at Aberdeen and dropped anchor. Blair lit lanterns to illuminate the deck and Buchan sorted out some boxes for makeshift seats. He placed them in a circle while we got the rations ready. We fully intended to share the overflowing baskets with the crew who had, without the narcissistic personality of Dwell on board, become more friendly. Apart from the captain and his engineer, Blair, there was also the first mate, Stan, a small wiry man with large hands and a ready smile. I unpacked the two baskets and portioned out the meat pies, bread and cheese, sweet treats and fruit, whilst Duncan poured us all a glass of Caomhain wine. There was plenty for everyone. As the last light of the sun filtered away into night, Stan brought out a mouth organ and played some jolly tunes, and it was a pleasant end to the night. Then it was time to get our heads down for another day of travel tomorrow.

As I made myself a makeshift bed on deck, I saw Duncan and Sophie give each other a nod. Curious as to what they were up to, I watched as they suddenly stripped naked and dived into the black water of the harbour. As they splashed and frolicked in the icy North Sea water, I looked up to see Buchan frowning. He gave me a quizzical look, and all I could do was shrug. Rolling his eyes, he bade me good night and ushered his crew into their quarters below deck. Listening to the sounds of the kelpies enjoying their dip, I opened the travel trunk to see if some blankets had been packed. There were three rolls, which I took out, unrolled, and laid out as beds on the deck. I lay down on one, arranging my shawl as a blanket and soon fell asleep.

The following morning, after a quick breakfast at 5am, we were off again, chugging south to the great Athens of the North, Edinburgh.

I had never been to the city before, having only ever travelled to Glasgow, and I was keen to know more. I had only learned about Scotland's capital from books and, although we were on a mission of mercy, I was looking forward to knowing more of 'Auld Reekie'. From my schooling, I had learned that the city was dominated by the castle sitting on top a plug of an extinct volcano. A road known as the Royal Mile ran down through the High Street, past the medieval buildings and on to the stunning Holyrood Palace. The castle had once had a loch on one side of it, the Nor Loch, but this was drained to create fine Princes Street gardens and to build Waverley Train Station. In the 18th century, it was proposed to extend the city just north of the castle, and the New Town, with its fine town houses and shopping area, was built. Although smaller than Glasgow, Edinburgh was still a big place and impressive, to boot.

We docked at the port of Leith, the nearest harbour to the city, and while Duncan helped his cousin from the boat, I stood on the quay wondering what to do next. The quay was jampacked with cargo ships loading and unloading goods from all over the world. The cobbled waterfront was busy with a variety of humans and creatures hauling boxes, driving carts, and hollering to one another about the latest news. It was a busy, bustling place and I would be glad to get away from it. But I had no time to lament the lack of peace. I had just one thing on my mind: how on earth were we going to find Dwell in a city as large as Edinburgh? We had scoured the port looking for The Lady Georgina as the puffer docked, but could see nothing that even resembled her description. I suspected they had landed, offloaded their live cargo and left. So, what next? We knew he had the creatures; we knew he needed some sort of laboratory, so the first place on my mind to go to was the University of Edinburgh. I had once read somewhere that it had a very good zoology department, so that seemed to be the best place to start.

I told Duncan and Sophie as we disembarked and walked down The Salty Barnacle's gangplank to dry land.

'Where is this university and how will we get there?' he asked.

'We'll need to take a cab.'

I hailed the first one I saw on Constitution Street and the three of us squeezed inside, our luggage piled high on our knees. It was uncomfortable, but we had no choice. There were no other vehicles for hire that I could see. I gave the driver instructions of where to go.

The cab drove us up the bustling Leith Walk. It was full of life of all sorts, from humans and dwarves, to centaurs and fairies. All manner of people were represented there: shopping for food, bartering on the street, driving horses and carts, or cleaning the streets. It was a lively place, noisy, and the air was heady with horse dung and the smells of a nearby tannery. The road wound its way uphill and within fifteen minutes we found ourselves on the famous Princes Street with its beautiful gardens and fancy department stores. Turning left into North Bridge, the Hansom cab took us across the Old Town, past a variety of tall dwellings and shops and along to the university's campus itself.

The Hansom cab drew up outside a splendid gothic building on which large brass letters declared: The University of Edinburgh Zoology Department. Based in the city's George Square, the building overlooked a large area of greenery and trees known locally as The Meadows. While Duncan paid the driver, I approached a man at the door of the building. He was holding a bunch of keys and appeared to be the doorman or a janitor. I inquired as to who I should speak to in the zoology department and he said he would go and fetch Dr . William Cooper, the Dean of that faculty, for me. He eyed Duncan and Sophie suspiciously, then told us to wait in the exhibit room.

He led us into a large airy room full of wood and glass cabinets, and dead animals stuffed into jars. The room smelled of formaldehyde and beeswax. It was meticulously clean. As we waited, we each examined the various specimens on display.

'Why would someone do this?' Sophie asked as she stared at a two-headed lamb perfectly preserved in a large glass bottle.

'To study them, I suppose,' I replied. I looked over at her and saw her shudder.

'Ew, creepy.'

Duncan walked over to a large cabinet and stared inside. 'You don't suppose…?' He began. 'No, surely not.'

'What is it?' I joined him and recoiled when I saw the cabinet's contents. There were various human body parts floating in specimen jars. There were two hands, one of which was showing signs of some sort of disease, an ear, a foot and several noses. Four death masks purporting to be from murderous criminals (according to the information cards placed beside them) had also been carefully put on display.

'What were you going to say?'

'I wondered if they also preserved parts of creatures and fae .' He looked at me, disgust on his face.

I shrugged. 'I don't know.'

'It's barbaric.'

'It's science!' said a voice. We turned to see a man in his 50s with white hair and huge mutton chop sideburns approach, a look of distaste on his face. Tall, portly and wearing a smart black suit with a mustard-coloured waistcoat and red silk cravat, he was a striking figure.

'Miss Abercrombie , I presume?' he said, holding out a manicured hand. I took it and shook.

'And this is my friend, Duncan and his cousin, Sophie,' I said. He shook Duncan's hand and nodded to Sophie, who simply glared back. 'We're here to ask for your help, sir. We're trying to track down my employer, Dr . Thaddeus Dwell, the renowned cryptozoologist and explorer.'

'You've lost your employer?' Dr . Cooper had a refined Edinburgh accent and looked bemused.

'I was supposed to meet him at Waverley Railway Station,' I lied. 'And he never showed. I've come here because he will more than likely get in touch with yourself.'

'And why would he do that, Miss Abercrombie? Our fields are not the same.' There was something twitchy in his manner, and he did not want to meet my eyes.

'No, they are not, Dr . Cooper, but he will be looking to use a laboratory and may approach you.'

That got his full attention. Dr . Cooper's steely dark eyes bore into me, causing me to feel discomfort. I did not like when a man looked at me that way. It was as if he was trying to pry out any information he thought I had hidden in my head.

'Well, if you leave me your address, I will be sure to let you know if Dr . Dwell ever comes my way,' he replied. 'Now, if you'll excuse me, I have some work to be getting on with.'

'Of course.' It was then I remembered we had not yet secured some accommodation. I told him so. 'May we call on you again tomorrow?'

He looked taken aback, and I could see he was trying to think of a way he could dissuade us from returning. Then he smiled and said: 'Yes, you may. Now, can I see you all out?'

Outside of the university, I bemoaned the lack of information.

'Well, it was worth a try,' Sophie said.

'Do you think he was telling the truth about Dr . Dwell?' I asked as we walked away from the building. 'He seemed a little shifty to me.'

'I thought that too,' Duncan replied.

We discussed our next move and agreed to concentrate on finding lodgings for the night. I felt we would be better looking for rooms somewhere nearby and we found a boarding house on the corner of Launsdale Terrace and Lauriston Terrace. It was a tall townhouse with a tiny front garden and large bay windows. There was a sign outside stating there were rooms to let, so we knocked on the door. The owner, Mrs. Seagate, was a woman of middle age. Small and thin, hair piled high on her head and her face was stern and pinched.

'The door will be locked at ten o'clock sharp every night,' she said, leading us to our rooms on the first floor. 'And there will be no visitors to your rooms, understand?'

We each nodded. She put Sophie and me in one room and Duncan in a room on the floor above.

'I run a respectable house,' she explained as she unlocked a door and ushered us inside, leaving Duncan in the corridor. 'Gentlemen and ladies are kept separate unless married, of course.'

'Of course.'

'Now, if there's anything else you two ladies require, please let me know.' She handed the key to Sophie and went out into the corridor to show Duncan to his room.

The first thing Sophie did was sit on the double bed and

bounce on it. There was only one bed, and it seemed we would have to share. This was a little unsettling, but I had always shared my bed with my siblings and was used to the phenomenon. Sophie was not pleased with the arrangement and said so, but there was nothing we could do about it. She unpacked her weapons and placed them under the bed. I took off my hat, placed it on a side table, and went to the window to look out on the view of the Meadows and the university in the distance. It was then that I spotted a familiar shape scuttling across the street. It was Cassius Ironblood. I gasped and Sophie flew to the window to see what I was so upset about.

'He's Dwell's right-hand man,' I explained, grabbing my hat and stuffing it on my head.

'Where are you going?'

'I'm going to follow him and see if he'll lead us to Dwell.'

'But you need to wait for Duncan!' She called after me as I left the room.

'Tell him where I've gone. I can't waste any more time!'

# Chapter 12

I ran down the stairs of the boarding house, past an astonished landlady and out into the street. Getting my bearings, I
hurried over towards the Meadows. Avoiding the many strolling
nannies with prams, I soon had the little man in my sight. He
was hurrying towards the university, no doubt heading to the zoology department. He approached the building and went inside.
I was right: Dwell was approaching Cooper for his help and he
had sent Cassius to broker it. I casually walked past the building, looking at its tall gothic windows, hoping for a glimpse of
Cassius talking to Cooper, but could not see them. So, I strolled
away from the building, crossed the road and sat down on a
metal bench a hundred yards away. It gave me a perfect view of
the building and I waited there for some time before the dwarf
finally reappeared. In fact, I nearly missed him. He exited the
building along with a group of young male students and I would
have not seen him had it not been for his distinctive red coat.
Getting to my feet and staying some distance away, I followed
him along the street. He was walking at a fast pace, and it was all
I could do to keep up with him. After walking for half an hour,
he suddenly turned up into a residential road lined with large

sandstone mansions. I struggled to keep up as he made his way towards the bottom of the street, afraid that if I didn't get there in time, I would not see which house he eventually turned into. Puffing and panting, cursing my tight stays and heeled boots, I arrived at the bottom of the street just in time to see him open the metal garden gate of one house halfway down the road and disappear. Slowly, carefully, trying to be as inconspicuous as possible, I walked up the street to find out the number of the dwelling. It didn't have a number, but a name… The Oaks. I looked for a street sign. It was screwed onto the wall of the home next door and said Grange Road. I walked past and headed to the top of the road where it met Causewayside Street. I turned into it and made my way back in the direction of the university. I hoped. Not being familiar with the city, I took an educated guess as to the correct way and was relieved  when I found myself once more at the Meadows. Elated to have found Dwell at last, I hurried to our boarding house, where I received a harsh scolding from Duncan.

'That was a stupid thing that you did,' he said, pacing in front of the fire in the public drawing room. 'You could have been seen.'

'But I wasn't seen,' I said. 'I think that's where Dwell is holed up. Cassius wouldn't be here on his own. Dwell might even have the creatures secured in the basement or an outbuilding. We should return tonight to see if we can locate them.'

'I'll do it… alone,' he said. There was determination in his eyes and before I could protest, he added: 'You've done enough. These men are dangerous, Esther , you know that.'

'I do and that's why I think I should go, too. Someone needs to protect you.'

'That's Sophie's job.'

'But – '

'No arguments, Esther ,' he said. 'I don't want to have to worry about you while we're there.'

I did not know how to answer this. I was so angry. The fury took all my words right out of my head.

He must have taken my silence for agreement, for he said: 'It's decided then. Sophie and I will go back to the house to see if Dwell and the creatures are there. You will stay here until we return. Then we can discuss the best way forward.'

Of course, I railed against this decision. Had I not shown bravery before? I knew Dwell better than either of them and; I told them, I should be the one to go. But Duncan was having none of it. He said I had already done enough and that I should wait at the boarding house for them to return. Where were they going to house the creatures once they had them? I demanded to know. Who's going to look after them? What will they eat? What if they were ill or injured or near death and needed nursing? I bombarded him with all these questions and he stood there, doing nothing, saying nothing, and waited until I had finished.

'I'm not arguing with you, Esther ,' he said. 'You stay here, end of discussion.'

A big part of me wanted to storm off in a huff, go somewhere quiet to lick my wounds, but I stayed. Those creatures needed me and my ego would have to take a back seat until they were rescued. Then I could tantrum to my heart's content, if I so desired. I told myself this whilst sulkily listening to Duncan and Sophie making plans for the night. She and I were to secure a cart from somewhere, whilst he would purchase tarpaulin and rope. We couldn't very well cart four large loch creatures through the city of Edinburgh in the open, even if it was in the dead of night. They needed to be hidden.

Grabbing our hats and shawls, Sophie and I sought out Mrs. Seagate in the boarding house. We found her sitting in her parlour drinking a sherry from a small glass. She looked startled when we arrived and quickly hid the glass under her chair. She stood up and quickly smoothed down her skirts with agitated hands.

'Ladies, what can I do for you?' Her hand tidied a stray tendril of hair at her ear.

'Can you tell us where we might hire a cart, Mrs. Seagate?' I asked.

'What do you want one of those for?' She walked to the fireplace and took up the poker.

'We have some business to attend to,' I answered, hoping the vagueness of my reply might assuage her curiosity. She looked at me, nodded and began to poke at the smouldering embers in the fireplace.

'And what type of business might that be?'

'Our business,' Sophie growled behind me.

Mrs. Seagate looked at her in alarm and replaced the poker. 'Pardon me, miss, but I didn't mean to pry. I was just making conversation. There is no need to take that tone with me.' She stood, arms folded, and glared at us.

'And there is no need for you to know what our business is,' Sophie hissed.

I put my hand on Sophie's arm and gave her a look, hoping she would get the hint and stop talking. Then I returned my attention to Mrs. Seagate.

'What my friend here is saying is that we are here on business and we would like to keep our affairs to ourselves… if you don't mind, Mrs. Seagate.' I hoped my voice was soothing, placating, without us having to say any more. I did not wish to rile our landlady having, at the back of my mind, the very real fear that she would throw us out of her home. But she seemed to calm a little.

'I don't mind, I don't mind at all,' she replied, eyeing Sophie behind me. 'I was just making conversation, that's all.'

'I know that,' I replied. 'So, can you tell me where we might hire a cart?'

Mrs. Seagate pursed her lips. Her hand, dry and red from washing, went to her chin as she thought. 'I reckon your best bet is to go to Gavallar's down in Marchmont Road. He has a few carts you might be able to hire.'

'Thank you, you've been most kind,' I said. I grabbed Sophie by the arm and pulled her outside.

In the hallway, Sophie huffed and puffed. 'Well, that human was so rude,' Sophie muttered as we gathered ourselves together. I secured my hat with a pin and fixed my shawl about my shoulders.

'She was just being inquisitive,' I said, checking my reflection in the hall mirror. It was a large gold framed oval mirror hanging near the door.

'Hmph.'

The wind had gotten up, and I pulled my shawl tighter around my shoulders. Edinburgh isn't known as the windy city for nothing. Perched on an area a few miles from the North Sea coast, it was a magnet for the cold northerly winds. We walked away from the boarding house towards the street where Gavallar's yard could be found. As we went, we were aware of several billboards pasted on walls and fences promoting an event at the University's zoology department that night. I stopped to peruse one and gasped. Dr. Cooper was holding a talk on rare animals that night and their relation to cryptozoology, and the guest speaker was none other than Dr . Thaddeus Dwell.

'He told me he didn't know Dwell,' I said, pointing animatedly at the poster.

'Who did?'

'Him.'

Sophie inspected the paper and shrugged. 'I cannot read your human signs and symbols. What does it say?'

'It says that Dr . Cooper was lying to me when he assured me he was not acquainted with Dwell. This poster says Cooper is holding a talk tonight and that Dr . Dwell is the guest speaker. That explains why Dwell came to Edinburgh and did not sail south for London—he had a speaking engagement to do before he left Scotland.' I felt agitated by this new revelation. If Cooper knew Dwell, did that mean he was helping him? If that were the case, Dwell knew we were here. I turned to start back for the boarding house, coming to an abrupt stop when Sophie grabbed my arm and yanked me back.

'Where are you going?'

'I need to speak to Duncan.'

'We can do that in a little while. For now, we must secure a cart for the creatures. We cannot take them out of this hellhole any other way.'

'But, Sophie, this is important.'

'And so is the cart.'

Gavallar's was only a few yards away down a small alleyway between two tenement buildings. The yard was squeezed between the back courtyards of the tall blocks of sandstone flats and secured by a tall fence and double gates. One of the gates had a human-size door cut out of it and it was through this we went.

The yard was empty save for an older portly faun  sitting

on a stool next to a shack. He was dressed for work in brown corduroy trousers from which his hooves stuck out, a white shirt and a black moleskin waistcoat. His head was bare and two sharp horns protruded from his curly brown hair. He sat, legs stretched out before him, smoking a long clay pipe, surveying us with shrewd eyes as we approached. He removed the pipe as we drew closer.

'Now, what would two fine ladies like yourself be doing in a yard like this one?' he asked jovially.

Sophie looked at me and I stepped forward. 'Good day, sir, my I inquire if you have a cart, we might rent this evening.'

His small, dark eyes narrowed, and he frowned. 'Now, what would you need a cart at night for? All goods should be carried during the day like normal.'

'Yes, sir, I understand that's what normally happens, but we have to move some... um... large items under cover of darkness.' I did not know what else to say, and I hoped I hadn't raised his suspicions even more.

'Oh yes? Doing a midnight flit, are we?' He chuckled, his great belly wobbling in the dull light of the courtyard.

'Something like that,' I confessed and tried to be as womanly as possible.

'Sorry,' he said, getting to his feet, 'but I can't help you diddle some poor sod out of his rent.'

He walked towards the door of the shack and tapped the pipe on the doorsill. The still burning ashes spilled to the ground. I approached him, hoping to change his mind.

'Oh no, sir! It's nothing like that! Is it?' I turned to Sophie for help. She went immediately to my aid.

'No, it is not.' She looked at me to elaborate.

'No, sir, for you see it's like this...' I touched his arm, hoping that the gesture would make him take pity on me. '… my husband… he's a brute, a drunkard. He takes out his anger on me and the children.' I was lying, but I hoped he couldn't tell. 'He'll be at the pub again tonight. He drinks all the money he makes and gives us all terrible beatings when he comes home.'

'He does.' Sophie confirmed my lies.

Gavallar, for it was he himself, looked at me with genuine concern in his eyes. 'And you need a cart to leave him?'

'Yes, sir. My cousin here…' I pointed back to Sophie, '… is going to help me load the little bit of furniture I have and the children into the cart and help me escape this terrible, terrible man. Oh, I rue the day I ever set eyes on that ungodly creature.' I wrung my hands and hoped I hadn't over-egged it too much. I looked up and Gavallar's eyes were misting up. He took my hand and patted it.

'Have no fear, mistress,' he said. 'I will do everything I can to help. Now how big a cart will you be needing and do you need a carter to help you? I would offer myself, but Mrs. Gavallar is expecting me home tonight.'

'We need your biggest cart,' I replied. 'For I have a large piece of furniture, a sideboard. The only thing I have of my dear departed mother's, that I will be taking with me. As for a carter, my cousin's husband will drive for us, won't he, dear?' I said this to Sophie.

'Er…yes.'

Gavallar looked at Sophie and then back at me. 'Of course, I will rent you a cart. How long do you need it for?'

'Just for tonight,' I said.

'We will return it tomorrow,' Sophie added.

Gavallar rubbed his chin. 'Albie's returning the big cart back later this evening. You could have that.'

I took a small purse from a pocket in my skirts and took out some of the money Duncan had received from his father.

'How much would that be, Mr. Gavallar?' I asked, fingers ready to pluck out some notes.

'I can't be taking money from a lady like yourself,' he said. 'Especially one in such dire circumstances.'

'But I insist. I always pay my way.'

'Just get the cart back to me in good form by first thing to-morrow and we'll call it quits.'

I put my hand out, and he shook it. 'Thank you, kind sir.'

'Come back here at seven and I'll give you the cart.'

Cart obtained, Sophie and I went back to the boarding house. I was anxious to get back to tell Duncan what I'd learned from the posters. He needed to know.

Duncan was thoughtful when I told him about the posters. 'That's good to know,' he said. 'But it shouldn't interfere with our plans. Now that we know Dwell is going to be at this event, it might actually work to our advantage.'

'How so?' Sophie wandered over. We were in the drawing room of the board house. I sat on the sofa; Duncan was next to me and Sophie had been standing, staring out of the window. She sat on the armchair nearest to Duncan and leaned in.

Duncan grinned. 'Because it means we can bring our plans forward and take the animals whilst Dwell is away. Plus…' And he looked at me. 'It means dear Esther has a job for the night.'

# Chapter 13

So, that was how it was that I found myself walking across the Meadows just before seven that evening, dressed for an evening's talk on cryptozoology from a man I had grown to despise. After we had finalised our plans for the rescue, Duncan had insisted I needed to look the part for an evening with Edinburgh's great and good. Despite my protests that I could not get a dress made in time, he asked Mrs. Seagate for directions to the nearest second-hand clothing establishment and before I knew it, he and Sophie had me bundled into a Hansom cab and taken me to the shop.

It was a respectable establishment run by a Mr. Harold Ross, his wife and daughter. I explained to them what I needed a dress and shoes for and they brought out a selection of fine, previously owned gowns. I chose a sky-blue dress, a lovely tortoise shell hair comb and a small evening bag. Shoes were a little trickier, but Mrs. Ross soon found me a nice white leather pair that fitted me perfectly. Dress and accoutrements bought, we three dined at a nearby restaurant and returned to the boarding house a little before six to get ready.

At 6.45pm precisely, my hair beautifully coifed, my stomach

churning, I bade my friends farewell and stepped out of the boarding house. The evening was fine, and it was pleasant to walk alongside the leafy perimeter of the Meadows towards the university. The sun was still giving off some warmth, there was the scent of summer flowers in the air and somewhere bees were buzzing. It would have almost been magical had it not been for the very serious reason I was there. Despite that, I could not help but enjoy the admiring glances my lovely dress attracted from passers-by. For once, I felt beautiful.

The zoology department door was already busy when I arrived five minutes later; menfolk in top hats and tails attended to women dressed in silk and glittering with jewels . The road was choked with carriages and cabs, and it was with some relief that I made it to the front door without any mishap. I purchased my ticket from a small pale man at the front door and made my way inside.

The talk was being given in the lecture hall, so, hiding amongst the crowd, I entered. My job was to keep an eye on Dwell and make sure he didn't leave the event too early. This was to give Duncan and Sophie the opportunity to rescue the creatures. If it seemed like he was leaving, I was to create a distraction. What that distraction would be, I did not know, but I hoped I would not need to. The hall was busy, noisy; the air was heady with cigar smoke and expensive perfumes. The room was laid out as all lecture theatres were in those days. The lecturer standing in the centre of six rows of raised wooden seating laid out in a semi-circle. The seats were sectioned off with walkways, which allowed students and visitors to access their seats more easily. I sat at the back, to the left of the centre and next to one such walkway. I had to ensure I was as hidden as I could be from the lecturers (I couldn't risk being spotted), but could get out of my seat quickly if I needed to follow Dwell. In the centre of the room, a Magic Lantern had been set up facing the plain white wall opposite.

At seven o'clock, Dr . William Cooper made his entrance from the doorway of the lecture theatre to rapturous applause from his audience. They stood and clapped for some three minutes before I heard him ask them to sit. There was the thunderous sound of several posteriors hitting the wooden benches before the room stilled to an expectant silence.

Luckily for me, there was a rather large man sitting in the row in front of me, which meant I could easily hide from view and just peep out at the speaker. This I did several times. Beautifully attired in a black evening suit, D r . Cooper looked splendid and was obviously enjoying being in front of an audience. He talked eloquently, describing his role in the university and about the work of the zoology department. He noted some of the unusual finds he had brought back with him following an expedition to Africa and how that had benefitted man's understanding of the natural world.

'And that now leads me to my special guest this evening,' he continued. 'This man has made headlines throughout the world for his work in cryptozoology, which, as you know, is the study of mythical creatures. And he has proven that some of those we once thought a figment of collective imagination were, in fact, real. Ladies and gentlemen, please put your hands together and welcome a man who really needs no introduction… Dr. Thaddeus Dwell.'

The sound of a hundred people getting to their feet to cheer and clap and shout was explosive. And it took some minutes for the noise to die down and for the audience to take their seats again. I knew Dwell was well known, but I hadn't realised how popular he was, so popular that as he thanked Dr . Cooper for the introduction, people were shifting about in their seats and craning to see him better. This made it quite difficult for me. Several times I leant to the side to see around the gentleman in front, only to have my view skewered by someone else. At last, the crowd settled down to listen politely to everything Dwell was saying and, at last, I got to see the man who, until very recently, had been my employer.

Dwell was looking terribly pleased with himself as he recounted his life in cryptozoology. There were gasps all round as he related tales of his Derring-Do in his attempt to prove the existence of some poor creature or another.

'Isn't he marvellous?' A woman to my left quietly said to her companion. 'So brave. So handsome.'

I quelled the urge to put her right on that subject and waited patiently as Dwell continued his talk. He had brought a number of slides with him for the magic lantern and nodded to the operator to show the first one. Again, gasps all round as the image of a large hairy creature, rather like a giant otter, was shown.

'This is an image drawn from life by an excellent friend of mine, the artist, Graham Mollieux. It shows a male Dobhar-Chu, or water hound, in its natural habitat in the lakes and rivers of Ireland. I caught one only last year.'

The next slide was a photograph he claimed was a Chupacabra, taken during an expedition to Puerto Rico. The image was blurry, but seemed to show a cryptid with sharp teeth and spines growing from the top of its head to the tip of its tail. As Dwell waxed lyrical on the horrible stories local people told him about the Chupacabra, I leaned over to see around the man in front and espied Cassius Ironblood standing near the lecture theatre's door. The dwarf was scanning the crowd, looking, no doubt, for myself and Duncan. As his eyes flickered in my direction, I quickly hid again, pretending to be as rapt in Dwell's stories as everyone else was.

Dwell then began talking about some of the water creatures he had also spied on during his travels: the Ogopogo of Lake Okanagan in Canada, the Kusshii of Japan and the lake monster of Lake Seljord near Telemark in Norway. My heart sank and my stomach twisted. I knew what was coming next.

'Of course, all these cryptids are not as famous as one… one, ladies and gentlemen, we here in Scotland all know about and that is Nessie, the Loch Ness monster.' Dwell paused, drinking in the atmosphere. 'And I have some exciting news on that score.' Pause. From my hiding place, I could see he was allowing that to sink in before continuing. He had the audience in the palm of his hand. I thought frantically about what to do. If he told the audience of the existence of the real Loch Ness monsters, the creatures would never be left alone. 'Yes, ladies and gentlemen, I can now announce that an expedition (I have only just returned from) to Loch Ness has borne fruit. I can confirm that…'

'Fire! Fire!' I shouted. I had climbed down from the seating area and was standing around the back so as not to be seen by either man. 'Quickly everyone out! Fire! Fire!' There were gasps and screams all round. People got up from their seats and began to push towards the door.

'Ladies and gentlemen! Please remain in your seats! There is no danger. There is no fire.' It was Dr . Cooper. But the crowd wasn't listening, so intent were they on escaping the lecture hall in one piece.

'Ladies and gentlemen!' Dwell tried his best to bring them back, but to no avail. Within minutes, the lecture hall had emptied. Even the Magic Lantern man left and Dwell and Cooper were standing alone, looking furious. From my hiding place behind the seating, I could hear them talk.

'What the hell just happened?' Dwell wanted to know. He sounded angry. 'I was just about to make my announcement. This is not on, William .'

'I'm sorry Dr . Dwell, but someone shouted 'fire'. You heard them.'

'Yes, but who was that? And why would they do that just when I was about to make my big announcement?'

'I have no idea. A rival, perhaps?'

I heard Dwell grunt. There was a pause and, heart thumping in my chest, I held my breath as I waited for them to resume their discussion.

'Look, Dwell, tonight's event is obviously over. Why don't we retire to my club for a drink and we can work out how best to plan the announcement? We can rearrange it tomorrow or the day after.'

I heard a loud sigh. 'I suppose I have no other option, old boy,' Dwell said. I heard them walk out of the room. Very slowly, I walked around the back of the seats and nearly dropped dead from fright. Cassius was still standing guard at the doorway. I slid back out of sight and hoped he would leave soon. Then I heard him muttering to himself as he departed the theatre.

'Fire! Fire!' he cried, imitating my voice. 'Stupid humans!' His footsteps disappeared from earshot.

With a sigh of relief, I tiptoed out of the lecture theatre and quickly made my way outside just in time to see Dwell and Cooper getting into a carriage. Hailing a cab for myself, I told the driver to follow their carriage. I needed to ensure I kept Dwell in my sight at all times. I needed to ensure he did not return to his lodgings too early and catch my friends in the act of saving the creatures.

Little did I know, Dwell wasn't the only one being followed that night.

My worst fears were confirmed when Dwell's carriage did not head towards the city centre as I had hoped, but turned up towards the place where I knew he had his lodgings. Dwell and Cooper were not going to the gentleman's club after all, instead, Dwell was heading home. And there was nothing I could do to warn Duncan and Sophie. All I could do was continue to follow them.

'Can you drive past the bottom of this street and stop?' I called to my driver. I did not want Dwell to know I was following him, so this seemed like a good solution. My driver did as I bid. I disembarked, paid him some coins and carefully walked to the end of Dwell's street. Their cab had stopped outside Dwell's rented house behind the cart Sophie and I had hired from Gavallar. Two huge Clydesdale horses stood patiently in front of the cart, tethered to some railings. They snorted and stamped their feet as the two men disembarked. There was no sign of Duncan, nor of Sophie or even the creatures in the cart. That meant they must have been still inside the house. I watched Dwell and Cooper get out of the cab and walk up to the front door. Warrington opened the door.

'You're back early!' I heard him exclaim.

'It's a long story!' Dwell grumbled.

From my position down the street, I watched the three men go inside the house. My stomach flipped. Duncan and Sophie were in that house. I had no doubt about that. The cart was there. So, must they be? I hoped beyond all hope that they had not been captured. Dwell was sure to kill them.

'Well, there's only one way to find out,' I muttered as I ventured closer to the house.

Still in my evening gown and high-heeled shoes, bag on wrist, I crept closer. The bushes at the front of the house prevented anyone inside from seeing me approach, but there was still the problem of getting inside. I walked past the house to the end of the street and then turned left. The road took me along the side of Dwell's neighbour's house to a back alleyway that ran the length of the streets . This must be where the tradespeople deliver their goods, I thought as I carefully made my way along the cobbled road. I counted the houses to my left as I went along: one, two, three, four, five. The fifth house along was Dwell's. I carefully opened the tall wooden gate in the property's fence and slipped into the back courtyard.

Like many city gardens, the courtyard was not a garden, but a place where washing was done and hung out, where the servant's toilet was and where coal was stored in a huge bin. The back court was in darkness. The sun shone on the front of the house, causing a long shadow behind. So. it was relatively easy to sneak up on the back door without, I hoped, being spotted by the individuals inside. It was well past dinnertime, and I hoped any servants had retired to their rooms or had gone home.

The back door, a typical wooden affair with two window panels, was unlocked when I tried the metal handle. It turned easily and the door silently opened, allowing me access to a deserted kitchen. Sparsely furnished with a large range cooker, a table and some plain cupboards, there was no hint that anyone had been there recently, or even that day, and I wondered if Dwell had bothered to hire servants. I snuck up to the internal door and strained to hear if there was anyone around. Hearing nothing, I left the kitchen and climbed up a flight of steps into the back hallway. This led me out into the main entrance hall. A beautifully carved wooden staircase led upstairs and there were rooms on either side. Quickly establishing that these rooms were also empty, I was just beginning to climb the stairs when something made me stop in my tracks. Something was glinting in the thick red carpet. There, lying on one step, was a small silver brooch in the form of a fern. Sophie's brooch. I picked it up and put it in my evening bag. Well, I now knew Sophie and Duncan were definitely inside the house, but where? I continued my ascent, freezing at every creak and sound I heard.

When I reached the first-floor landing, I became aware of a muffled conversation coming from the other side of a closed door. I bent down to listen, trying to make out what was being said, but could not do it. I knelt down and placed an eye on the keyhole. What I saw made me gasp.

Warrington was standing with his back to the door and brandishing a knife and talking animatedly to someone inside. His large frame was blocking the view of his audience, but when he moved to one side, I knew instantly what had befallen my friends. Duncan was tied to a wooden chair, his hands bound behind him, his mouth gagged, one eye heavily bruised and swollen. Beside him, tied to a second chair, Sophie was unconscious and sagging to one side. Her face also had the marks of violence. As I watched, Warrington grabbed her by the hair and yanked her head back. He seemed to be trying to ascertain whether she was genuinely unconscious or faking it. When she did not react, he let go of her hair and her head lolled forward. Duncan, red-faced with fury, screams muffled by the gag, struggled at his binds. He had a murderous look in his eyes. But his feeble attempts to free himself only caused Warrington to laugh and sneer.

I must do something, I thought as I turned around to make it easier for me to get to my feet. It was then that I saw the pistol pointed in my face and the sneering, snarling visage of Cassius Ironblood.

'Good evening, Miss Abercrombie,' he said. 'How good of you to join us.'

# Chapter 14

How did you…? I mean…'

'I followed you from the university. You were so busy trying not to be seen by Dr . Dwell that you failed to watch out for anyone tailing you.' The dwarf looked far too pleased with himself. 'Such a stupid girl, always a stupid girl. Now, get to your feet and open that door. Mr. Warrington will be delighted to see you.'

He jabbed me in the back with the pistol and made me open the door.

Warrington snorted when I walked into the room, arms up, the dwarf with a gun at my back.

'Guess who I found spying on you, Mr. Warrington?'

'Miss Abercrombie! Well, now I have the trio. Are you something special too?'

I looked at him, puzzled by what he meant and then I realised. He must have found out that Duncan and Sophie were kelpies . But how? I looked at Duncan, whose anger had turned into fear. Fear that I had been captured and would be tortured too. I took a deep breath, and fighting my own terror, addressed Warrington.

'Let my friends go, Mr. Warrington, and I'll tell the police you helped,' I said, my voice quavering slightly towards the end.

Warrington laughed a great big belly laugh. 'Don't be a fool, girl. I have no intention of letting any of you go.'

'Well, the police will be here any minute and they will arrest you along with the rest of them.'

Warrington studied me. I felt his pale grey eyes probe me as if he were trying to find out whether I was lying or not. I tried to hold that cold gaze, but it was impossible, and I found myself looking away.

'You're lying,' he said. 'There are no police. You've come here all on your own, haven't you?'

I looked him straight in the eye and bit my lip.

'Haven't you?' he snarled. When he got no answer, he turned to Cassius. 'Go check for me, will you, Mr. Ironblood?'

The dwarf looked irritated at this request, but bowed and left the room. Warrington returned his attention back to me. 'Now, what are we going to do with you?'

He came at me then with a murderous look in his eyes and in my fright, I could do nothing but back away. I felt my back hit against a side table and my hand scrambled for something to defend myself with. My fingers closed around a small, but heavy picture frame. I grabbed it and threw it at his grinning face just as he thought he had me. He roared and dropped the knife as the silver frame struck. Then he lunged. I ducked, and I ran around him, accidentally kicking the knife in the direction of Duncan and Sophie as I did. It was a fortunate thing too, for I was able to scoop it up as I ran.

'Come here, you little…!'

Warrington was after me again. I ran around the back of Duncan, placed the knife in his hand and darted to the other side of the room, the huge hunter hot on my heels. I squealed as he grabbed for me, his meaty hands grasping empty air as I dodged. I ran for all my life was worth.

'Stand still, you fool,' Warrington roared as he lumbered after me. He chased me around an occasional table, knocking a lit oil lamp to the floor. The oil spilled all over a threadbare Persian rug on the floor, igniting it and forcing Warrington to pause in order to stamp it out.

'What are you trying to do, girl? Kill us all' He puffed as he stomped on the flames. Fire swiftly put out; he returned his attention to me.

It was just at that precise moment that my luck ran out due to a miscalculation on my part.

Eyes blazing with anger, a sneer on his lips, Warrington stomped towards me. I ducked to the left; he blocked me. I ducked to the right, again he blocked me. I found myself backing away into a corner, ignoring the pain as my thighs brushed against the corner of a small table. Seeing I was trapped, the sneer turned into a manic grin, and Warrington kept coming. I found myself in the very far corner of the room next to an alcove with shelving full of books and nick-nacks. I pulled a small marble statuette from the shelf and held it in front of me, reading to strike when he was close enough. Eyes full of scorn, a smirk playing about his nasty lips, Warrington raised his huge hands and closed in. I threw the statuette at him, but with a swipe of one powerful hand he batted it away. I grabbed a book and threw it too, but again he managed to divert it. I desperately looked around for something else, but couldn't see anything in time. I closed my eyes and crushed my body as hard against the wall as I could, silently praying this would be over soon.

Bang.

I heard the thud followed by a groan. I opened my eyes just in time to see Warrington fold, eyes rolling, tongue lolling, as he collapsed to the floor. I looked up in shock to see Duncan standing before me, a silver candlestick in his hand. He was grinning. I leapt over Warrington's body and into his strong arms, giving him an excited kiss on the lips as a thank you for saving me. He dropped the candlestick with a clunk, put both arms around my body, and leaned in for a more intense kiss. He pressed his soft, soft lips to mine, and I felt myself melt into his hard body. My legs went soft, and it was all I could do to keep myself standing. After what seemed like an age, he pulled away, leaving me flushed and panting.

'You saved me,' I said. My voice was breathless and my heart was beating wildly.

'You saved me. I'm just repaying the compliment.' He was smiling, and I couldn't help but smile back. Then moaning from behind him brought us abruptly back to real life. Sophie was coming round.

'What happened?' she moaned as she opened her eyes. Duncan rushed to her side and, using the knife, cut her free of her bonds.

'Warrington got us,' he explained, deftly sawing away at the rope that held her. 'Esther , here, came to find us and she rescued us.' The rope burst, and Sophie brought her arms around to the front to give her wrists a rub. Duncan got to work on the ropes binding her feet. As he did so, Sophie looked at me. There was gratitude in her green eyes.

'Thank you Esther ,' she said. 'I owe you one.' Shakily, she pulled herself to her feet

'It wasn't all me,' I said. 'If Duncan hadn't hit Warrington with the candlestick, I would be sitting next to you.'

'He deserved everything he got,' Sophie said, looking down at the stricken hunter. She gave him a vicious kick in the side. 'Mhac Na Galla!'

'Sophie!' Duncan chided.

'What did she say?' I wanted to know. Sophie was standing there over Warrington, smirking.

'She called him a son of a bitch!'

'Ah.'

'Wh-a-a-a-t?' Sophie said innocently. Then she kicked the hunter again. 'He deserves it.'

A sound coming from the hallway alerted us that the dwarf was returning to the room. We could hear him singing a dwarf battle song as he approached the door. Duncan hid behind the door, whilst Sophie grabbed some rope and stood on the other side of the door. They waited until the little man entered.

'There's no police. The girl was lying,' Cassius said as he opened the door and walked into the room. 'What the -? What are you doing?'

It was then that the kelpies pounced. Duncan grabbed him and pinned his arms whilst Sophie worked to tie him up. The little man struggled and yelled for all he was worth. It all happened so fast all I could do was stand dumbstruck in the middle of the room.

'Gag him before he alerts Dwell!' Duncan shouted to me. I looked around for something worthwhile. Seeing Warrington had a necktie around his neck, I quickly knelt down and unwound it. Then I ran to the dwarf and stuffed it in his fat little mouth. The dwarf glared at me as Duncan put the finishing knots on his binds. Cassius spat the tie out.

'You'll pay for this, girl!' he yelled at me. Dunk. Sophie had picked up the fallen candlestick and hit the little man on the

LOCHNESS

head. He lost consciousness immediately.

'You haven't killed him, have you?' I gasped.

Sophie felt for a pulse. 'No, he's just out. Horrible creature that he is.'

'Esther , help me tie Warrington up before he revives,' Duncan said. While we did that, Sophie secured the gag in Cassius' mouth and sat the little man on an armchair. Bound up like a Christmas goose, he looked almost comical lying there. But there was no time for laughter, for we still had to find Dwell and the creatures.

Once Warrington was secure, we convened at the door to discuss our next move. Sophie and Duncan believed they were keeping the creatures in the basement. It made sense; the creatures were ungainly on land and moved rather like seals. They would never be able to climb the stairs and were too heavy for anyone, even someone of Warrington's great size and strength to carry.

'They have to be there,' Sophie said. 'It's the only place we haven't yet searched.'

A clock on the wall struck eight as we descended the stairs in a single file. It was still light outside, the late evening sun sending shafts of light through the front windows of the house. In another hour or so, it would be dark. We did not have a lot of time to free the creatures and get them on to the cart before the sun went down. We hurried down to the ground floor, well, hurried in the only way three people who did not want to be heard could… carefully and quietly as possible. At last, we reached the ground floor and looked for the door that would lead us into the basement. We found it at the rear of the property in a small windowless ante-chamber that was accessed through a door in the kitchen. I had passed it earlier and assumed it was a cupboard.

163

We gathered inside. Then Duncan put his hand on the door and looked back at us. It was then, in the dull light of that tiny room, that I noticed he seemed to be flagging.

'Are you alright?' I whispered. 'You've gone very pale.'

He nodded. 'I need to get to water soon,' he said. He looked up at his cousin, who was also beginning to wilt. The kelpies had been out of water for too long. If we didn't act fast, if we were at all delayed in this rescue, they could become seriously ill.

'Maybe we should come back,' I said. Duncan shook his head. 'But – '

'It needs to be today…now,' he said. 'We'll be fine.' He looked again at Sophie. 'Ready?'

'Ready.'

Duncan led the way down a set of wooden stairs, closely followed by Sophie. They were unarmed except for Sophie's Sgian Dhus and dirk, which she had retrieved from Warrington before we had left. She had the Sgian Dhus; Duncan wielded the dagger. The stairs creaked beneath us as we made our way down to a large open room lit by gas lighting and candles. It was some sort of makeshift laboratory, full of shelving, with various bottles of brightly coloured liquids, scientific equipment and tools. There was a large wooden table, the kind you would normally find in a kitchen, in the centre of the room, on which sat a microscope and various slides. A leather-bound notebook sat open nearby along with a dip pen and ink. A pair of gold-coloured round spectacles had been placed on the notebook and a half-eaten sandwich lay on a small plate next to a used teacup and saucer. Where is he? Duncan mouthed to me. I shrugged. We moved to the edge of the table and studied the notebook. It was full of Dwell's observations about the creatures and rough drawings of their physique. Just then, we heard the sound of someone whistling. A door in the far end of the room opened, and a startled looking Dwell, in shirtsleeves and a leather apron, walked in carrying a bucket of water. He started when he saw us. Then he put the bucket down near the door and quickly regained his composure.

'Well, well, well, if it isn't Miss Abercrombie and her merry band of…' He looked Duncan and Sophie up and down and waved an insolent hand. '… whatever you two are!'

'Dr . Dwell,' I stepped forward. 'You have something we want back.'

He gave me a nasty smile. 'I can't think what that could be, dear Esther ,' he said, running a hand over the edge of the table as he walked closer. He paused a few feet away from us, grinning, but it was short-lived. His face fell when he spied Sophie peering at his microscope. She put out a hand to explore the instrument better. 'Don't touch that!' he barked. Her hand recoiled, and she glared at him. 'That's very delicate. I can't have just anyone touching my equipment.'

Sophie backed away and stood. Dwell relaxed and returned to me.

'Now, if you don't mind leaving, I have some experiments to do.'

'We're not going anywhere.' Duncan stepped in front me. He was pale, but looked strong, the dagger in one hand at his side. 'Not without the creatures.'

'What creatures?'

'The ones you took from my cave.'

'I have no idea what you are talking about. Now, leave before I call my man.' Dwell stepped up to the table and took the sandwich from its plate. He bit into it and chewed nonchalantly.

'Do you mean Mr. Warrington or Mr. Ironblood?' I asked.

Now it was my turn to appear casual. 'Because they are, unfortunately... indisposed.'

Dwell stopped munching and glared at me. 'If you don't leave now, I will be forced to send for the police,' he growled 'You are trespassing on private property.' Then his eyes flickered to a coat-stand I had missed when we entered, a coat-stand on which his jacket hung.

Curious to know what had drawn his attention to the jacket, I walked over and, despite his protestations, rifled through the pockets.

'I say! That's my jacket! Get your filthy hands out of there.'

Dwell took a step towards me, but was prevented from going any further when Duncan lifted the dagger and held it at his throat. His pockets seemed to be empty, so I tried the inside ones and found a small iron key in one. I lifted it out and held it up. Dwell's face fell.

'What does this open?' I asked.

'Nothing.'

'It must open something, Dr . Dwell, or why else carry it about your person?'

'If you must know, it's the key to the front door,' he replied. He looked away, and I knew then that he was lying.

'Or maybe it opens something else,' I said. 'What was in the bucket you were carrying?'

'What? Nothing.'

I walked over to where he had left it and examined it. It was full of water, fishy smelling water. 'Was there fish in this?'

Dwell's lips tightened. 'I don't have to answer your questions,' he said.

'Sophie, could you keep an eye on Dr . Dwell for us, whilst Duncan and I go and look where this door takes us?' I asked.

'Gladly.' Sophie drew a Sgian Dhu and held it to Dwell's person whilst Duncan and I slipped through the doorway into a corridor.

The corridor was small and dark. Having no natural light, using the light streaming through from the laboratory, we could just make out a second door. Taking the key, I slid it into the lock and turned it. The lock opened. With a quick glance at Duncan, I opened the door. It slid open easily and inside a tiny room, dimly lit with a Tilly lamp hung on a hook overhead, were the four  terrified looking creatures. They blinked in the dim light and cooed when they saw Duncan. They were tied by the neck to large iron rings on the wall and their attempts to go to him were quickly thwarted by their bonds. On seeing this, he rushed to them and with the dagger sawed away at the cord around Athair's neck.

'It's alright, friend,' Duncan said softly as he freed the patriarch of the group. 'I'll soon have you all back home.'

Athair then came up to me and nuzzled my hand. He seemed to sense we were there to help him and his family. Within minutes, an exhausted Duncan had all four  free, and we led them out into the laboratory. Ungainly on land, it took them a few minutes to squeeze through into the laboratory.

Dwell flinched when he saw us taking his prized creatures.

'Put them back, those are mine!' he growled. It was at that moment that Sophie, who had gone an alarming shade of puce, suddenly dropped her blade and staggered against the table. Before she could compose herself, Dwell seized his chance. He picked up the weapon, grabbed Sophie, spun her around so that she had her back to him, and held it to her throat. He grinned maniacally.

'It seems I have the upper hand,' he said. Duncan made to

move forward but was stopped when Dwell tightened his grip on poor Sophie, causing her to cry out in pain. 'Ah! Ah! Just stay where you are. Now, here's what's going to happen. You are going to return the creatures to their room and you are going to join them. I'll have Warrington deal with you all after I've found out what you did to him. I'm sure he'll want to take out his revenge. In the meantime, all three of you can stay in that stinking room with these...' He looked at the four  creatures in disgust. '... things and...'

Before he could finish what, he was about to say, Duncan gave out a loud keening sound. It was so loud; I had to put my hands to my ears. The sound echoed off the tall ceilings of the laboratory and made Dwell wince. After a few seconds, he could no longer stand it either. He let go of Sophie and the Sgian Dhu and grabbed his head. At the same time this happened, Duncan rushed to Dwell's side and punched him hard. Dwell spun on his feet and went down like a bag of  potatoes. Duncan then collapsed to the floor, exhausted and desperately needing the restorative powers of water. Without thinking, I rushed over to the bucket full of stinking fish water, picked it up, and used it to revive both kelpies . It wasn't enough to fully restore them, but it might be enough to allow them to escape the house and last until we could get back to Leith and open water.

Duncan grimaced and spluttered when the water hit him on the face. I did the same to Sophie and soon both kelpies  had regained consciousness and enough strength to help me herd the creatures up the narrow stairs to the front of the house. It wasn't easy. The animals had the dexterity and size of a walrus, but, as we gently coaxed first Athair and then the other three  up the steps, we managed to get them outside.

We got them to the cart before Duncan and Sophie could

physically do no more. I made a makeshift ramp from two planks of wood we had put in the cart for the purpose and shooed and cajoled the beasts up into the back. I covered them with a large tarpaulin we had brought for the purpose, whispering to them to stay hidden when they raised a head or peered out from under the sheet. Then I helped the exhausted Sophie and Duncan into the driver's seat. Fearful they would fall off; I secured them both by tying a rope around their waists and securing them to the seat. I climbed on board, took the reins, and was about to give them a flick when I saw a man emerge from the house. It was Cooper. I had forgotten all about him. He must have been hiding in the house while we were rescuing the Loch Ness animals. He gave me a scared look as he scuttled down the garden path and out into the street.

'I wasn't here, Miss Abercrombie, understood?' he said, eyes darting along the street. 'I want no part of this.' He looked up at me. 'I thought Dwell was telling a tall tale when he said he had captured the Loch Ness monster. I just came here to humour him. I had no idea he planned to dissect them. My career would be in tatters if people found out I had links to him! Please, tell no one I was here.'

I looked down at him from my seat on the cart and nodded. Looking relieved, he silently thanked me and then turned tail and hurried off down the street. I had no axe to grind with Dr . Cooper and was just relieved that we had managed to save the creatures. I looked down at the great wide backs of the two Clydesdales in front and then gave the reins a flick. Because of the weight of the beasts in the back, the cart horses moved off slowly down the dim street. I glanced back once and could see no sign of Dwell or anyone else in pursuit. We had done it.

Slowly, carefully, we made our way across the city, now quiet save for the odd carriage and carousing drunk. It was dark now and the street lanterns had been lit. The horses' hooves made clip-clopping noises on the cobbles as they made their way down to South Bridge, on to North Bridge, across the Royal Mile and down into Princes Street. We took a right and travelled for a bit more before reaching the top of Leith Walk. We took a left, and the horses made their way down the long street that would take us to Leith and open water.

All the time we were travelling, I continued checking on my companions. Duncan was barely conscious; Sophie was totally out of it. They were close to not waking up at all and desperately needed to be in the water. I hoped sea water would be just as good as fresh and was anxious that we would not get to the dock on time. And then there were the creatures. They were quiet in the back, hidden as they were under the tarpaulin. They had not looked in good shape either. I had to get them all into the water, and fast. However, the horses were struggling with the weight of the cart and the increasingly steep incline of the road. We had started our journey at a decent pace and were now down to a slow walk. I couldn't do anything about it. I had to keep going.

Half an hour later, we had reached Leith docks. The place was in almost total darkness, save for a few street lamps illuminating the main thoroughfare. I looked around to see who was about and might see the peculiar sight of a heavily laden cart moving about the city at that time of night. There were a few sailors drunkenly making their way to a nearby tavern. So intent were they on getting inside, they did not notice as we clip-clopped past. Some ladies of the night roamed in the shadows, paying us no heed. On seeing the sailors go into the bar, they followed them. The pub door opened, spilling light and the noise of many voices outside. Then it closed again, and all was quiet. A policeman walked by on his beat and paid us no attention. He disappeared off into a side street. Then the street was silent.

We reached the harbourside a few minutes later.

'Duncan! Duncan!' I climbed down from the cart and walked around to help him from the driver's seat. He mumbled something incoherent. 'Wake up. You need to help me,' I said, untying the rope from around his waist and pulling him towards me. He fell sideways, his weight slumped against mine, and it was all I could do to stop him falling and hitting his head on the cobbles. I guided his body to the ground and then, mustering the last of my strength, grabbed his wrists and dragged him to the quayside. I rolled him towards the edge and pushed him into the water. There was a splash, but I resisted the temptation to go and look for him. I had another person to save first. I hurried to Sophie and did the same with her. She was a little lighter than Duncan, but it took everything I had to haul her to the sea. I pushed her in and watched as her body hit the black water and disappeared. And then I waited. Nothing. I grabbed an oil lamp from the side of the cart and held it up. The dull light played on the softly lapping water, but there was no sign of Duncan or Sophie. Was I too late? Had they both died and their bodies been dragged into Davy Jones' Locker? My stomach knotted at the prospect of never seeing Duncan again. Despite my best attempts to ignore my growing feelings for the kelpie , it was only then that I finally admitted that I truly loved him. Tears welled in my eyes as I searched the inky depths for any sign of them.

'Come on, come on,' I muttered to myself as I stared at the water. 'You can't be gone.'

I watched the water for the best part of ten minutes, willing them to appear, but there was nothing. Not a ripple. Fear gripping my insides, I stood back from the edge and thought about what I should do next. How was I going to transport the four creatures back to Loch Ness? I couldn't do it alone. I had no money, no friends, and no idea of where to start. Just then, something broke the surface of the water and gasped. I rushed to the edge of the quay and held the lamp aloft to see Duncan grinning. There was another splash, and Sophie joined him.

'I am so glad to see you both,' I gasped. Relief must have poured out of me, for Duncan commented on it. 'I was so worried you had both died,' I explained. 'I don't know what I would have done if you had.'

The look Duncan gave me was hard to interpret. It danced between sheer pleasure and abject worry, and that concerned me. Something was going on with him. Did he know how I felt about him? I hoped so. He had kissed me several times now. Did he feel the same? He had never said, but those kisses were so full of tenderness and want that it was impossible not to think he had feelings for me too. But we didn't have time for that right now.

Sophie must have seen the look between us, for she interrupted it with: 'I don't know what's going on between you two, but we don't have any time for that. We need to get those animals into the water before they perish.'

I put my hand down so that she might grab it and I could help haul her out, but she shook her head. Instead, she swam to the side of the quay, grabbed a hold of a wooden ladder secured to the side and got herself out. Duncan soon followed, and they soon stood dripping on the quayside. I immediately went to Duncan's side, intending to embrace him, but his aloof manner put me off. I looked at him, puzzled and unsure of what had suddenly changed. He would not look at me.

'Come on, let's get this lot into the water,' he said, pushing past me and hurrying towards the cart, 'before anyone sees what they are.'

As he and Sophie rolled back the tarpaulin, I placed the two planks against the back of the cart so that the creatures might use it as a ramp.

'How are we going to get them back to Loch Ness?' I asked as the first creature carefully negotiated its way down the make-shift ramp.

'We're going to swim them back,' Duncan said.

'Can you do that? Aren't they fresh-water animals?' Surely the sea would make them ill, I thought as the second creature disembarked from the cart.

'Normally, but they have adapted to be able to live in both,' Sophie explained. She led the creatures to the quayside and paused. She turned. 'Thank you for everything you have done, Esther Abercrombie. Your help will not be forgotten.'

With a quick wave, she dived into the water and was soon followed by the first three creatures. I stood for a moment, unsure what that meant. Was that it? Was that how Sophie was going to say goodbye?

'Help me with him.' Duncan climbed up on to the groaning cart to shoo the third creature, the big male Athair, from the cart. 'He's reluctant to get off.'

As we worked together to coax the animal off, I snuck a glance at Duncan. His face was drawn. He was worried about something. When Athair was on the quayside and wriggling towards the water, he finally turned to me. Still dripping wet, he grabbed me by the shoulders and gave me a kiss on the forehead.

'Sophie and I are going to swim in the ocean with the creatures,' he said. 'Can you make your way back to Loch Ness on your own? There is money in my room. Can you pay our landlady and bring my things?'

'Of course, I can.'

'You need to leave the city quickly. Dwell is a dangerous man. He could come after you and we are not here to save you.'

'I will be fine, Duncan,' I replied. 'I'll start my journey north first thing tomorrow.'

'Good, then I will see you there in a few days.' He turned and walked towards the quayside.

'Duncan!' He turned and looked at me questioningly. 'Be careful!'

'You too!'


I was left alone on the dark docks, unsure now of where I stood with my kelpie friend. Our parting had not been what I had expected. When had the decision been made for Sophie and Duncan to swim home? Had they even thought about how I was going to get back? Maybe I was just being selfish. After all, the entire trip had been about saving the creatures…and we had successfully done that. Hopefully, things would be better when we met again at Loch Ness. Well, I'd best get these horses and cart back to the yard and turn in, I thought as I turned around.

I gasped. Dwell was standing beside the cart, looking furious.

# Chapter 15

So, we meet again, Miss Abercrombie!' he sneered. 'You have been one pain in my backside. I regret the day I ever hired you to be my secretary.'

He walked towards me, and I found myself backing up against the side of the quay. One more step and I would plummet into the inky depths of Leith Harbour, something I did not relish in long skirts and a corset, despite being a good swimmer. I could do nothing else but stand my ground.

'What do you want, Dwell?' I said. There was no fear in my voice. I was feeling strong. Powerful. 'You've lost. Get over it.'

'I may have lost the battle, but I haven't lost the war.' He was nearly upon me. 'I'm going to kill you now and then I'm going back to Loch Ness to kill your companions. And then I going to get my creatures back.' I desperately looked around for a weapon. The only thing I had was the cart lantern that was still in my hand.

Dwell took a knife from his inside pocket and caressed it. 'You know, I've never cut up a human before.' He looked at me. 'Perhaps you can be my first. It will be an excellent revenge.'

'You don't want to do that,' I replied. My foot felt the edge of the stone quay. I looked behind me to see the dark waters glint in the light of the lantern.

'Oh, I think I do,' he sneered. Then he suddenly lunged at me and I did the only thing I could do. I threw the lantern at him. It smashed against his jacket, the oil spilling out all over him, the lit wick igniting it, igniting him. He screamed and dropped the knife. Dancing around trying to put the flames out, he looked over to the water and with one great leap, jumped. I heard an almighty splash and looked to where he had gone in. In the dull moonlight, I could just see him surface.

'Help! Help!' he called. 'I can't swim!'

'Hold on!' I replied, looking around me for some rope. Rope! The cart! I rushed to the side of the cart and dug out the rope that I'd tied Sophie and Duncan with. I went back to the water's edge just as Dwell's head went under the water. His hand was still reaching up, so I threw the rope towards it. He tried to grab it, but missed, so I threw it again. He resurfaced, gasping for breath, and I tried again. Just as I thought he had caught it, a large dark shape appeared in the water beside him. It coasted past him, turned and went back. What the hell is that? Before I could do anything, before I could pull him out of the water, a huge serpent's head broke the surface next to him. Dwell screamed and tried to swim to the harbourside, but he couldn't get away from the monster quick enough. The creature opened its mouth wide, displaying a cavern of perfectly sharp teeth and two long fangs. As quick as a flash, it pounced and swallowed Dwell whole. The last I saw of him was his feet disappearing into the rancid depths of the creature's throat, a pool of blood blooming on the water and a large shiny tail disappear under the surface. It was over in seconds.

'What the -?' Then I remembered Dwell's obsession with

cryptids and his desire to see one in particular, the Sabre-fanged Anaconda of the Atlantic Ocean. 'Was that a…? It wasn't, was it?' From his description of the creature earlier in our acquaintance, I was sure that was indeed what it was. Well, he had gotten his wish. He had finally seen one. I shuddered. What a horrible way to die.

I did not linger long at the quayside for fear I would be blamed for Dwell's untimely death. So, I walked over to the cart, climbed on to the driver's seat and gave the reins a flick. The horses moved off slowly, and I made them do a wide arc to turn the cart around. Picking up the pace, I drove them to Leith Walk and headed back towards the city centre. Retracing my earlier route, I made my way back to the yard to drop off the horses and cart.

Gavallar's gates were closed, but I had been instructed to knock loudly and the night watchman would let me enter. I did this and left my vehicle with a grumpy-looking elf watchman.

I walked back to our lodgings.

The building was in darkness and silence when I opened the front door. A solitary candle in a little brass candlestick stood on a dresser in the hallway. It gave me enough light to see the stairs. Exhausted, I hauled myself up to the first-floor landing and found the room Sophie and I had been sharing. I opened the door and went in.

Falling on the bed still fully dressed, I slept heavily until morning. It had been a long and hard couple of days and I needed the rest.

I awoke the following morning to the chimes of the grandfather clock in the hallway. I counted eight and decided it was time to get up. I rose, stiff and sore from the previous evening's exertions, and stripped out of my gown. There was still water left in the ewer, so I poured it into the basin and washed. I changed into fresh clothing, my white blouse and brown travelling skirt, tidied my hair and slipped out of my room. Although hungry, I had one thing I had to do before going downstairs to breakfast and that was clearing out Duncan's room.

His room was on the floor above, and he had given me his key for this purpose. I slipped inside, gathered what little things he had left into my arms, and placed them on the bed. Kneeling down at the side of the bed, I felt under the mattress for the stack of money I knew he had hidden there and pulled it out. This I stuffed down the front of my corset for safe keeping. Once again gathering Duncan's knick-knacks—a comb, a tooth-brush and a small leather pouch to keep them in—I returned to my room and put them with my own things in the travelling trunk. Then I went downstairs and breakfasted on smoked fish kedgeree and tea.

Mrs. Seagate kept several booklets listing the times of trains, omnibuses and other forms of local transport on a display cabinet in the dining room, and it was these I consulted. There was a train leaving in half an hour from Waverley Station to Perth. From there I could get the Inverness train. Once I arrived in the Highland capital, I would work out my next move: how to get back to Drumnadrochit and Strone. I would work that out later. For now, I had to catch this train.

I rushed upstairs, put on my jacket, and placed everything into the trunk. There was nothing to collect for Sophie. She seemed to have been carrying everything when she left. I fastened my hat to my head, took a last look around, and dragged the trunk downstairs. Then I went to find Mrs. Seagate to pay her.

Waverley Station was busy with commuters when I arrived

by Hansom cab twenty minutes later . I had been lucky to have
been able to find the cab so quickly outside my lodgings. But it
wasn't until it dropped me inside the station that I began to feel
I was actually going to be able to catch the train. Instructing a
porter to carry my trunk, I hurried inside the squat station building and purchased my ticket. Then we rushed to platform six,
where the train was already waiting. It was a large black steam
train with four carriages. Porter in tow, I ran to the first-class
carriage and, after paying the man for his trouble, got on with
my trunk. I quickly stowed it away on some shelving and then
sat in the compartment. I had never travelled first class before,
having never had the money, but I soon settled down for the
journey ahead, relieved to be heading north at last. I felt elated and worried and tearful all at once. I knew Dwell could not
bother us anymore and that the creatures were safe, but my poor
heart was aching with longing for Duncan. He had seemed distracted the previous evening, and I hoped that didn't mean he
was no longer interested in me. My thoughts were momentarily distracted by the banging of carriage doors being shut and
the shouts of the platform staff. A whistle screeched. The train
chugged, shunted forward, and then moved off from the station. I looked out of the window to watch as the platform, with
its high sides and smoky atmosphere, slide out of view. Then
we were travelling through the city and out into the countryside.

I removed my notebook from the trunk and tried to get
down some of our adventures of the last few days. It helped me
make sense of everything that had happened and distracted me
briefly from the fear that Duncan was no longer interested in
me. However, it wasn't long before my thoughts drifted back to
him. What had that chaste kiss on the forehead meant? Did he
think of me as a friend? As his sister? I wanted so much more.

I loved him. My heart yearned for him. My mind could think of nothing but his beautiful brown eyes and strong manly figure. The very thought of him sent my body tingling with excitement. And yet…there was this nagging doubt at the back of my mind that something had changed. In the time it took from us being at Loch Ness to the time we freed the creatures, Duncan had gone from a loving, attentive man to someone distracted and distant. Had Sophie put him off me? My stomach flipped with fear.

The train drew into Perth a few hours later and from there I caught the first train to Inverness. I arrived in the late afternoon and could not secure transport to Loch Ness until the following day. Finding myself having to stay in the town overnight, I secured my lodgings in a small, family-run hotel and dined in a café next door.

The following day, I set off again, a passenger in a fishing boat travelling down the Caledonian Canal to Loch Ness, where they would drop me off at Strone. The boat would then continue down the loch, re-join the canal at the other end to travel westward.

It was a warm and sunny day when we left Inverness, but I could not enjoy the weather as I sat on the fishing boat's prow, worried about Duncan. Despite my best efforts to put these bleak thoughts from my mind, I could not escape the feeling that I might never see my kelpie again.

Mrs. Mackenzie seemed pleased to see me when I stepped inside the bar area of the inn shortly before lunchtime. She bade me sit down at a table and disappeared into the back, returning a few minutes later with a bowl of soup, some bread and a cup of tea. Placing them down in front of me, she sat down on the chair opposite.

'Did you get them?'

'Yes.'

'Are they alright?'

'Yes.'

'And they're back here?'

'I don't know,' I replied. I looked around me and leant over the table. In a lower voice, I told her that Duncan was bringing them home by sea, but that I wasn't sure if they had already arrived.

'I've not seen him, not since the day you two left,' she replied.

Just then, the door of the bar opened. I jumped at it. But I was sorely disappointed when one of her regulars walked in. She stood up.

'That's good news, anyway,' she said with a wink before leaving me to eat my meal. 'Morning Wully, the usual?' She called as she went behind the bar again.

Anxious to see if Duncan, Sophie and the creatures had indeed arrived home, I ate my meal as quickly as possible and went upstairs to my room. Mrs. Mackenzie had kept it for me. The room was as I had left it. My small travelling trunk was in the corner, my book on the dresser and my nightgown on the bed. I sat down on the wooden chair near the window and took stock. My stomach lurched when I thought of Duncan, my hands trembled and I wasn't sure if I wanted now to seek him out. My mind had examined and re-examined everything that had happened the previous day, and I was now sure he wanted to end it.

'Well,' I said aloud, mustering every bit of courage I could find, 'there is only one way to find out.'

I quickly changed into a fresh dress and went to check my reflection in the mirror on the dresser. The face that stared back at me was hollow-eyed, tired, and pale. I pinched my cheeks to bring back some colour and tried to smile. What reflected back was a wonky fake grin and worried eyes, but it would have to do. I put on my hat, gathered my shawl, and left.

The day was bright and dry, but overcast, and under normal circumstances, it would still have been a nice walk to Duncan's home. However, my heart was heavy and the fear of rejection gripped my very being. How I would be able to go on living without him, I did not know, but, I reasoned, it was better to know than not. I forced myself to walk past the castle, through the copse of trees, to the base of the hill where his cave was. Clambering up the tiny path, I entered the cavern.

'Hello? Duncan? Are you here?'

Silence.

I walked into his living quarters feeling awkward for being there, but desperate to see him to get all this worry and anticipation over with.

'Duncan? Hello?'

The room was empty. Perhaps he was at the underground loch. I lit a lamp, then slipped through the curtains into the cold stone passageway and followed it down to the hidden cavern. The place was eerily quiet. There was no snuffling of creatures, no splash of play, no soft warm bodies and… no Duncan. He can't be home yet. I felt a ruffle of relief that was quickly replaced by worry. What if something had happened to them? No, he was a kelpie ; he was used to the sea and the lochs; he was fine. It's just taken them longer to get here.

I retraced by steps to Duncan's living area, blew out the lamp and left. Perhaps he was at that moment swimming up to the jetty to find me, I thought, as I negotiated the path back down to Urquhart Castle. Yes, that was it. But it was not Duncan's handsome face that greeted me when I returned to the inn, but someone I had no wish to see again.

# Chapter 16

C assius Ironblood was standing in the doorway puffing on his pipe when I approached the building. I paused a few metres away, unwilling to take a step further while that odious little man was there. He saw me, gave me a look of disgust and then stared out towards the far side of the loch.

'So, you're back then?' he growled.

'I came to retrieve my things,' I replied. Unwilling to show him he still unnerved me, I walked towards him.

'Huh.' Then he said. 'That's what I'm doing here. I'm packing up and taking Dr . Dwell's equipment back to London. I will meet my master there and we will regroup.' He looked me dead in the eye. 'Don't think this is over, Miss Abercrombie. Dr . Dwell will return to these shores to catch the creatures again.'

'I wouldn't be too sure about that.'

'What do you mean?'

'Dr . Dwell won't be hunting any creatures in the future.'

He gave me a quizzical look. 'What have you done to him?'

'I didn't do anything. He did it all himself.'

'Explain.'

And so, I told him about Dwell attacking me on the quayside and him falling into the water. I told him how I tried to save him, but couldn't because of what happened next. I described the snake-like creature that suddenly appeared in the water and how it took Dwell to his watery grave. Cassius seemed unmoved by the news. He shrugged.

'I told him to be careful around the waters of Leith. It's a favourite hunting ground of the Sabre-fanged Anaconda,' he said. He put the pipe back in his mouth. Then he smiled. 'I can think of no better end for that man.'

'I thought you – '

'Liked him? No. I just worked for him. He paid well, but I suppose I'll not get my wages now.' He looked over to where the barn was. 'Now, I'm wondering what to do with all his things.'

'If I were you, I would take it in lieu of wages. I'm sure there are some butchers who would buy your knives and some people who might take the carriages.'

He nodded.

'Promise me one thing,' I said, 'don't sell it to people who would hunt the creatures. Let them be.'

He looked up at me and grunted.

I went back up to my room to think about what my next move should be. I decided I needed to stay until I knew Duncan was safe and well. Then I would see where things stood with him before working out what I should do next. I, too, was now short on my wages. By working with Duncan against Dwell, I had effectively put myself out of a job. I looked in my purse. I still had the money Duncan had given me, but that I would return to him as soon as I could. All that was left were a few coins I had for myself. I had enough to pay for another night at the inn and maybe a train fare back to Glasgow, but that was it. I had to make a decision soon. I walked to the window and looked out. The loch was quiet and still as glass. There was no sign of the kelpies or the creatures. Where are you Duncan? I thought.

To keep my mind off worrying, I decided that what I must do is to be busy, so later that afternoon I offered myself as a helper to Mrs. Mackenzie. At first, she seemed unsure. She could not offer me wages, she said. I set her mind right on that point.

'I just need to keep busy just until I know he's safe,' I said. 'Please, it'll help me.'

'Alright,' she said, pleased with our deal, 'can you cook?'

'Yes.'

'Well, there are dinners to be made and glasses to be washed. Adam will help you.' She looked at her son, who made a face.

I gave her hand a squeeze. 'Thank you.'

And so it was that the inn got a new staff member for the night and just as well for the bar was busy with customers new and old. We finished up just past midnight and wearily gathered in the hallway to wait while Mrs. Mackenzie locked up. She was just turning the big old iron key in the front door when a loud hammering startled us all. Glancing back at us, fear in her eyes, the landlady slowly opened the door and then laughed. She turned back to me. My stomach did a somersault.

'He's back.'

Duncan stood in the dull glow of the oil lamp, looking all handsome and sheepish. As Mrs. Mackenzie and her son discretely withdrew after leaving me instructions to lock up, Duncan invited me outside for a moonlit walk beside the loch. It was a beautiful, still night. The only sound was the gentle lapping of the waves and a light breeze that ruffled my hair. The moon was full, illuminating our way, and the evening was cool. Duncan took my hand and led me down to the small jetty where the puffer had once tied up.

'I'm so glad you're safe,' I said holding the oil lamp in one hand. 'I was beginning to worry something terrible had happened.'

'Nothing bad happened,' he replied with a small smile. In the light of the lamp, I saw him bite his lip and then he looked at me with those lovely eyes of his. 'Esther , we need to talk about what's been happening between us.'

I stayed silent. He looked out over the water and somewhere an animal called.

'I think that maybe we were starting to take a path that would not work out well for either of us,' he continued. He looked at me again, his hand warm in mine. 'What I'm trying to say is that I've started having feelings for you…'

'I have too!'

'…no! Let me finish…I have feelings for you, but we can't take them any further. It would be foolish, dangerous.'

I removed my hand from his and took a step back. 'What? Why?'

'You are human. I am kelpie . It is unheard of that we should be in a relationship.'

'But, you did it before, with Janey .'

'Yes, and look how that turned out.'

I turned my back to him and pulled my shawl tighter around my shoulders. The worst had happened. He was breaking up with me. I felt his hand on my shoulder. Gently, he turned me around.

'I'm sorry, but I just can't risk it. Kelpies and humans were never meant to be together. It's just the way it is.'

'What brought this on? We were so happy together. Did Sophie talk you out of being with me?'

'No, it was not Sophie. I've been thinking about it for a while, and when Warrington attacked you, I knew you would never be safe with me. It is best that you stay with your own kind.'

'But I love you, Duncan.' It was out before I could stop it.

'I know, but you'll find someone else. A good human man who will take care of you and give you lots of babies.'

'But I don't want another man.'

The doleful look in his eyes almost broke my heart. 'I'm sorry. It is how it has to be. Goodbye Esther Abercrombie and thank you for everything you have done for me and for the creatures. I will never forget you.'

He took my free hand in his, raised it to his lips, and kissed it. Then, with a last nod of his head, he disappeared into the darkness of the night, leaving me bereft on the shoreline. It was then that the tears came, a great flood of self-pity and heartbreak. I could not imagine a life without him, could not fathom how I was going to go on. A sound startled me and I looked up to see Cassius grinning at me. He shook his head and then walked away.

His reaction must have triggered something in me, for I went after him, anger coursing through my veins. I caught up with him and, with one shove, pushed him to the ground.

'What was that for?' the little man said, leaping to his feet and brushing himself down.

'For laughing! Oooh, I'm so done with men!' I screamed at him. 'All of you!'

I hurried back to the inn, got inside, and slammed the door. Locking it, I took the oil lamp upstairs and nearly ran into Mrs.

Mackenzie, who was standing on the landing looking concerned.

'It's over,' I said, rushing past her. 'And I'll be leaving in the morning.'

I did not wait for her reply, but handed her the lamp, ran into my room and shut the door. I threw myself on the bed and sobbed myself to sleep.

I returned to Ayrshire the following day, catching the first train I could from Drumnadrochit station to Glasgow and from there on to Ayr. Mrs. Mackenzie gave me a parcel of food and a bottle of beer to have on the way and saw me off. One of the local men was taking me to the loch-side village by row boat. He stood at the pier whilst I said my goodbyes.

'Thank you for everything, Mrs. Mackenzie,' I said.

'You're welcome back anytime,' she said, giving me a hug. 'Thank you for saving our creatures,' she whispered in my ear.

On the train, heart heavy, I took out my novel and threw myself into the story again. Despite a crushing feeling in my chest, I resolved to return home with my head high and my spirits unbroken. So, my love affair had gone wrong. So what? My family would never know about it. But what would I tell them about the job? I decided to tell them some of the truth, that Dr . Dwell had unexpectedly died and that the job was over. They would be thrilled that my adventure was over and that I was now ready to settle down in our farming community, meet a nice boy, and get married. No, not married. I couldn't see a future where Duncan wasn't in it. Well, maybe I would become a schoolteacher or a live-in governess. I could teach. I would be good at it. I couldn't see myself returning to work on the land, but those options didn't seem too bad.

By the time the train drew into Ayr Station, my spirits had lifted somewhat. I was back home, ready to be welcomed into the rowdy bosom of my family again. They did not know I was returning, so no one met me, but that was okay with me. I had a little money and planned to arrive home in some style. I paid the postman to taxi me home in his horse and cart.

When we drew up to the front gate of my small cottage early that evening, warmth and gladness filled my heart. I was home. My great adventure was over. Time to live in the real world.

'Thanks Bert,' I said, climbing down from the Post Office cart and removing my luggage. I paid him a shilling and waved him off. Lugging my small travel trunk through the front gate, I put it down on the neatly paved pathway and looked up to survey my childhood home. It was small, but well kept. It was cosy and full of love. All the windows were open, for it was a fine night and I could hear voices within.

'Anyone home?' I called.

A face appeared at a window. It was Dougal, my youngest brother.

'Esther? Esther's home!'

Within minutes, my entire family, with the exception of my father and two of my older brothers, were swarming out of the cottage and engulfing me in their arms. It was all I could do to stay still as the sun-brown arms latched themselves around me one after the other, my mother last of all.

'What brings you home early, lass?' she asked when my siblings finally let me go again. 'Not that I'm unhappy to see you back. Quite the contrary.'

'It's a long story, Mum,' I said.

'Well, long stories are always best told over a cup of tea. Come on, let's get you inside. Dougal, bring the trunk in, will you?'

I wasn't sure how much I could tell my family, so I embroidered the truth. I told them Dwell had died in an accident (truth) and that I had met a man I had fallen for (truth), and that it hadn't worked out. I left out the dangerous adventure I had been on or the fact that Duncan was a kelpie . They would have been shocked and horrified that I had put myself at risk like that and would not have understood the love I had for a creature, especially one that was supposed to be mythical. They would have called Duncan a monster and wouldn't have been quite so understanding and loving about my broken heart.

I spent the next few days recovering from my experiences in the bosom of my family. As I got used to sharing a bed again with my two sisters and the boisterousness of a full house, I reflected on how lucky I was to be part of such a loving family. With their animated conversations and gentle teasing, they helped me heal a little from a love affair I thought I'd never be over. They saw I was sad and did everything in their power to cheer me up, from saving me the last bit of jam in the jar to having me sit closest to the fire at night. Dougal even went as far as to collect some wild flowers and present it to me as a 'cheer you up' gift. He is so sweet, my youngest brother.

Slowly, I felt the heaviness of my heart soften. A week passed by and I began to feel I was functioning more like myself again. Two weeks, three and I was laughing with them all again, helping out around the farm and seeking out a new position, preferably nearby. After a month, although I would never forget him, the impact Duncan had had on my sorrowful heart was beginning to lessen.

And then it happened.

It was a Sunday afternoon and; it being the day of rest; the family was all about the farm reading books or sketching or knitting in the parlour. The animals had been fed and cleaned out before church and, once the service was over, the day was my own to do as I pleased. I chose to take a walk along our local beach. It had been a habit of mine growing up and I picked it up again on my return home. There was something soothing about the feel of the salty air on your face, the cold sand under bare feet and the knowledge that you had this lovely stretch of sand all to yourself.

I set off straight after lunch. My intention was to spend the next hour walking and thinking before returning to finish my latest novel. Removing my boots and stockings, I luxuriated in feeling the cool, soft sand underfoot. It reminded me of my childhood, that had been carefree and full of laughter. My siblings and I had often come down to the beach of a weekend to play and lark about in the waves. I walked towards the water's edge where the sand was at its dampest and looked for interesting shells and sea-glass. As a girl, I had collected these and was still on the look-out for something more unusual for my collection. I suppose that was why I did not notice the dark head in the water, nor the tall, athletic figure rise out of the waves. The seagulls called overhead. The waves lapped. But I was only interested in the corners of white shells peering out of the sand, just daring me to dig them out. I was not aware Duncan was there until he spoke.

'Esther.'

I did not react for, truth be told, I had often thought I'd heard his voice over the past four weeks, but they had all been aching hallucinations. So, assuming I was just hearing things again, I went about my business wading through the shallow water at the beach edge and picking up pretty stones and what-nots.

'Esther.' His voice was louder, more insistent. I turned around and there he was, soaking wet and handsome in only a pair of trousers and his silver chain glinting in the sunlight on his chest. The very sight of him brought all those tortured weeks flooding back. I felt sick. 'Well, aren't you going to say hello?'

'Hello Duncan,' I replied. I could not believe my own eyes. Here he was, Duncan, the former love of my life, standing in front of me, dripping with sea water and tormenting me again. I resisted the urge to run into his arms. Instead, I turned away from him and began to stroll down the beach again. I tried to act casual, but inside my whole being was in turmoil. How dare he turn up like this, out of the blue? How dare he think I could be civil to him after he had discarded me, had broken my heart? I needed to put physical distance between us, so I walked away. I felt his hand grab my arm, and I stopped.

'Esther , it's me, Duncan.'

'I know who it is,' I said, turning around to face him. 'What do you want?'

'I… er…' I must have been giving him a hard look, for he grew flustered under my gaze.

I was not about to give him an easy time. If he could not spit out what he had come to say, I was not interested. I had to protect myself. 'Goodbye Duncan.' I started walking off again.

'No, wait! I need to speak to you… please!'

I paused, thought about it and felt I should hear what he had to say. 'You have five minutes.'

'I came to find you because I have something important to say,' he began. I looked up at him and found myself longing to kiss those soft lips again. Damnit! Chiding myself for being stupid, I tried to concentrate on what he was saying. 'I miss you, Esther . I miss you terribly and I can't live without you. Please, will you give me another chance? Can we start over?'

What was he saying? That I should forgive him for breaking my heart? That I should just fall into his arms again as if nothing happened? 'You hurt me, Duncan. You set me aside and didn't give our relationship a chance,' I began. 'I've been home for a month now. If you really missed me so badly, why didn't you come and see me before now?'

He looked down. 'I was trying my best to forget you.' He looked me in the eye. 'I thought if I put distance between us, the love I have for you would die and I could live my life in peace and happiness again.' He blinked. 'But that didn't happen. Everywhere I went, everything I saw reminded me of you. I kept imagining you coming out of the inn and walking down to the water's edge, the breeze ruffling your beautiful hair.' He bit his lip. 'I love you Esther . I have loved you since the first time I set eyes on you that night outside the inn. Please, will you give me another chance?'

I studied him. He seemed in earnest, but I wasn't sure I could go there again. My heart was still bruised and bleeding. I couldn't take another disappointment.

'I'm not sure… I can't think straight…' I turned about and began walking back the way I had come, leaving him standing on the wet sand behind me. 'I need some time,' I called back.

'I'll be waiting,' he said.

My mother was standing at our front door when I arrived home. She had been gathering some flowers from the garden to put in a vase in the kitchen and had paused when she heard me coming. She frowned.

'Are you alright, Esther ? You look a bit pale.'

'I'm fine, Mum .' I walked by her, but she stopped me with a hand on my shoulder.

'What's the matter?'

'Duncan is here.'

She looked up and around us, eyes filled with fury. 'Where is he? I want to give him a piece of my mind.'

'He's at the beach, he's apologised, said he had made a mistake. He wants us to get back together.'

'And what do you want?' I could feel her question pierce my heart.

My eyes filled with tears. 'I don't know. I love him, but I don't want to get my heart broken again.'

'Come here.' I felt her arms encircle my shoulders, and she pulled me in for a hug. 'Only you can make the right decision. Only you know your own heart.'

I nodded.

'What's this Duncan like? Is he a good man?'

'Yes.'

'Would he provide for you?'

'Yes.'

'Can you see yourself living without him?'

Here I paused. 'No.' My voice wavered.

My mother pulled away and wiped my tears with one hand. 'Love hurts, but if it's the right love, it can be wonderful,' she said. 'You have a choice: you either go to Duncan or you don't. It's entirely up to you. However, don't just make a snap decision because you are still feeling hurt. You don't want to make the wrong decision and regret it.'

'There's something else I haven't told you.' I paused. How could I break this gently?

'Don't tell me he's married?'

'No, not that. It's just that... he's... well, he's not human.'

'What is he? An elf? Fae? A dwarf?'

'None of those, mum. He's a kelpie .'

LOCH NESS

'A kelpie ? Well, well, well, so my father was right. They do exist.' She bit her lip.

'You're not angry?'

She smiled. 'Why would I be angry? Humans fall in love with different species all the time. There's nothing wrong with it.'

'But what will dad say?'

'He'll be happy so long as you are happy,' she replied. 'So, am I right in thinking you have made a decision?'

I sighed. I thought about it for a few seconds. What did I actually want? Was it just fear holding me back? Could my love for Duncan overcome that fear? I looked at my mum and smiled.

Duncan was sitting on the beach looking nervous when I returned to him. He stood up and brushed himself down as I ran up and threw myself into his arms. As he wrapped his big strong arms around me, I kissed him passionately on the lips.

He pulled away and said: 'Does this mean what I think it means?'

'Yes, I want us to be together,' I replied. It was the only thing I wanted. Being without him over the past few weeks had been agony. I never wanted to be away from him ever again. I kissed him again. 'I never want us to part ever again.'

'Will you marry me, Esther Abercrombie?'

I looked into my beloved's brown eyes and smiled. 'Yes.'

We returned to the farmhouse so that I could introduce Duncan to my family. My father was out, but my mother was home and welcomed Duncan warmly. She gave him some of my elder brother's clothes to put on whilst his trousers dried and had him sit at the kitchen table whilst she bustled about making tea. I sat next to him, nervously waiting for my father to come home. As she laid out the tea things on the table, she asked us how we met. She asked about Duncan's background, his family,

195

where he lived. She told him funny stories from my childhood, making me blush down to the roots of my hair. We did not tell her about the crazy adventure we had been on together and how it had brought us together. To tell it would mean revealing the truth about the Loch Ness Monster, and that would never do. While I trusted my mother, I could not trust any of my siblings. They would blab to their friends and before we knew it, there would be sightseers and pressmen crowding Loch Ness. We had to protect the creatures at all costs. We weren't lying to her; we were just not telling her the whole truth.

'So, Esther says her employer sadly died,' my mother said, pouring hot tea into her best china cups.

Duncan glanced at me and then back to my mum. 'Yes, he had a terrible accident in Leith, I believe.'

'Such a nasty way to go.'

'Yes.'

Just then, the kitchen door opened, and the huge frame of my father blocked the doorway. He looked at Duncan and frowned.

'Dad!' I said, getting up from the table. 'I'm so glad you're here. Can I introduce you to my... to Duncan?'

My dad, eyeing Duncan warily, took a step forward and thrust out his hand. Duncan got to his feet and shook it.

'Pleasure to meet you Mr... er,' my Dad said.

'Mackintosh.'

They shook hands heartily for what seemed like minutes, before my father let go and went to sit at the table. My mother poured him a cup of tea.

'Please call me Duncan, Mr. Abercrombie.' Duncan returned to his own seat.

'I can't be doing that,' my father replied. 'I don't know you well enough to be so familiar.'

Duncan looked at me. 'Well, actually, Dad…' I began.

Duncan stood up again. Dad frowned. 'Sit down, lad, and have your tea.'

'Actually, Mr. Abercrombie, may I speak to you somewhere in private?'

My dad looked at Duncan like he wanted to kill him. 'What for?' He took a sip from his cup.

'Please, sir.'

With an audible sigh, my father rose from the table and showed Duncan out into the garden. While the two of them spoke, my mother and I crept up to the window and watched. They were standing outside the perimeter of the fence on the public road, having an earnest conversation. My father was talking animatedly and appeared to be grilling Duncan. I felt pity for my Duncan then, for I knew my father was a tough negotiator, but my beloved seemed to be holding his own. After what seemed like an age, they shook hands again, turned and began to walk back towards the house. Quickly, my mother and I resumed our seats at the table. The back door opened, and the men strode in. My father looked grim. Oh no, I thought, as he took his seat silently. Duncan did not look at me, but returned to his place, too. I looked from one to the other, desperate to find out what had happened. Then my father burst out laughing.

'I can't keep this up any more,' he said.

I looked at Duncan and saw he was smiling.

'Well, go on then, tell the missus what you just asked me,' Dad said.

'Mrs. Abercrombie, I have just asked your husband permission for your daughter's hand and he has agreed.' Duncan reached over and took my hand. He gave it a squeeze. 'We're going to get married.'

I could tell you everything that went into the preparations for that wedding, which took place the following spring, but that is a story for another time. Needless-to-say, my mother was delighted with the news and she brought out a bottle of good whisky for us all to toast the good news.

My father held up his whisky glass. 'To Esther and Duncan,' he said. 'May their marriage be blessed with many children and happiness.'

'Children?' I looked at Duncan. I hadn't thought about children. 'Do you want to have children?'

'At least five, maybe more,' he replied.


THE END



Some Scottish words:

Aye = yes

Loch = lake

Firth = a narrow inlet of sea, an estuary

Smirr = light rain

## ABOUT THE AUTHOR

Dawn (D A) Nelson is an award-winning Scottish author of books for both children and adults. She writes action-packed romantic thrillers and dark comedies for adults as well as fantasy adventures for kids. Apart from writing for the SOS series, Dawn is also planning a fantasy/steampunk series for adults too. Her first book was a kids' novel, DarkIsle, which won the Royal Mail Scottish Children's Book Awards (8-12 age group) in 2007.

Dawn lives in a small country village on the banks of the River Clyde, just a stone's throw away from the beautiful Loch Lomond. She lives there with her two kids, three small dogs and three chickens. In her spare time, Dawn loves to read and enjoys both literary, romance and fantasy books. When not writing or reading, Dawn loves to bake and watch movies.

Sign up to Dawn's newsletter: https://danelsonauthor.com/

**Social Media**

Facebook:  https://www.facebook.com/authordanelson
Twitter:  https://twitter.com/danelsonauthor
LinkedIn:  https://www.linkedin.com/in/dawn-nelson-95210221/
Tik Tok:  https://www.tiktok.com/@danelson70
Pinterest:  https://www.pinterest.co.uk/danelsonauthor/
Goodreads:  https://www.goodreads.com/author/show/1351494.D_A_Nelson

# OTHER BOOKS BY D A NELSON

## BOOKS FOR ADULTS

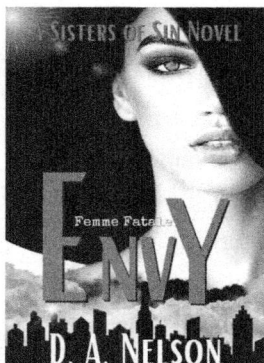

**Envy**

Envy loves her life as an assassin working for the Sisters of Sin...until her ex, Adam, shows up begging her for help. Someone's forcing children into slavery on African cocoa plantations.

Pretending to be a couple, Envy and Adam fly out to the Ivory Coast to investigate.

What they find sickens even her...and now she's armed and very, very angry.

The sixth in an eight-book female assassin series written by a team of international authors, Envy has it all... Enemies to lovers. Action and adventure. Fake relationship. And hot, steamy sex.

**https://geni.us/envydanelson**

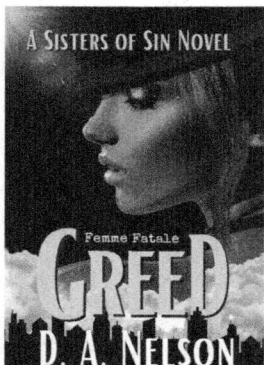

**Greed**

Berlin. Present Day.

It's a fact of life that opposites attract. So, when SOS assassin Alex Greir, aka Greed, bumps into Nick Walker in a Berlin nightclub, sparks begin to fly.

An MI6 agent, Nick's been sent by the British Government to infiltrate the Sisters. But, one look at the beautiful

Alex and he's smitten. He's got a new mission now: to tame the feisty blonde and make her his own. However, the gorgeous Alex has other ideas. She's no pushove for a handsome face. Then she finds out wh And all hell breaks loose.
Gripping, sexy and electrifying, this is the story of Greed.

Amazon: **https://geni.us/cI4I**

All other ebook retailers: **https://books2read.com/u/bz159q**

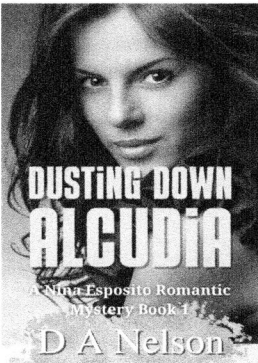

### Dusting Down Alcudia

Nina Esposito, archaeologist, is on a mission. She's flying to Mallorca to locate a magnificent Roman treasure that's been lost for centuries.

But, when a former love and a work rival vie for her attention, Nina finds herself locked in romantic roller-coaster. Which one is truly worthy of her? And do they have ulterior motives other than winning her heart?

Added to the mix is a Spanish billionaire who will stop at nothing to get the jewels for himself.

Who will get to the treasure first? Will Nina's heart be broken along the way? And can she really trust either of the men in her life?

Join Nina on a breath-taking journey of discovery that takes her from the dusty fields of Mallorca to the diamond brokers of Amsterdam. As she soon finds out: there's everything to play for when you're Dusting Down Alcudia.

**https://geni.us/alcudia**

**The Jacobite's Share**

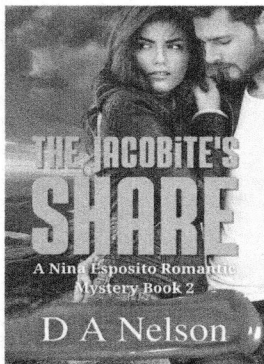

When an argument leads to estrangement from lover Jay, Nina decides to take a research job at a Scottish castle to get away from her troubles.

Back in her native land, the plucky archaeologist soon finds herself up to her ears in a centuries-old mystery and attempted murder.

Now she's got to find the Jacobite treasure before a would-be assassin picks off the handsome Laird and his equally gorgeous brother... a brother who has taken quite a shine to her.

And when Jay returns to her life, things will only get further complicated as his ex-fiancée shows up to create mayhem.

The second in the popular Nina Esposito Adventures, The

Jacobite's Share is a fast-paced adventure thriller full of darkness and danger.

https://geni.us/jacobitesshare

## Everything She Wants

When married Susan decides to run away with a Wham! tribute band as their 'Shirley', little does she know of the consequences it will bring. Fed up with her cold husband, desperate to get away from their spoiled teen daughter, she joins the group to find some happiness in her life. And she gets it - for a while. As the group gets more successful, Susan finds herself falling for an 80s pop heartthrob. Has she finally found true love and will she get everything she wants?

https://geni.us/everythingshewantsbook

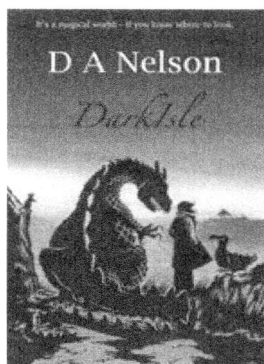

## BOOKS FOR KIDS (8-12 years)
## THE DARKISLE TRILOGY

### DarkIsle

For 10-year-old Morag, there's nothing magical about the cellar of her cruel foster parents' home. But that's where she meets Aldiss, a talking rat and his resourceful companion, Bertie

the dodo. She jumps at the chance to run away and join them on their race against time to save their homeland from an evil warlock named Devilish, who is intent on destroying it. But first Bertie and Aldiss will need to stop bickering long enough to free the only guide who knows where to find Devilish: Shona, a dragon who's been turned to stone. Terrifying, touching and funny, DarkIsle is a vivid and fast-paced novel of captivating originality.
**https://geni.us/darkislenovel**

**DarkIsle: Resurrection (The Witch's Revenge)**

The 2nd book in the DarkIsle trilogy. Two months after she saved The Eye of Lornish, Morag is adjusting to life in the secret northern kingdom of Marnoch Mor. But dark dreams are troubling her and a spate of unexplained events prove that even with the protection of her friends—Shona the dragon, Bertie the dodo and Aldiss the rat— Morag is still not safe from harm... The 1st book (DarkIsle) WON the 2008 Scottish Children's Book Awards.
**https://geni.us/darkisleseriesbook2**

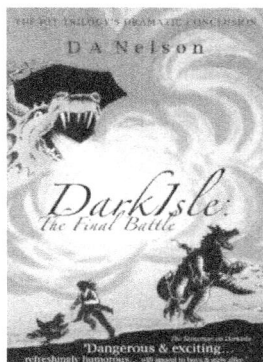

**DarkIsle: The Final Battle**

All seem well in Marnoch Mor. Bertie the dodo, Aldiss the rat and Shona the dragon are looking forward to a relaxing Christmas. However, Morag is having bad dreams – an old enemy is trying to reach her. And when another former foe turns up on her doorstep it is clear something is badly wrong.

Morag and her friends are soon forced to face a powerful new threat, one more terrifying than they have ever encountered before.

The battle for the DarkIsle of Murst must be won…or Marnoch Mor itself will be lost.

https://geni.us/darkisleseriesbook3

**A Children's History of Glasgow**

Have you ever wondered what it would have been like living in Glasgow when William Wallace was there? What about being a sailor on one of the ships owned by the rich tobacco lords in Georgian times? This book will uncover the important and exciting things that happened in your town. With a helpful timeline, fun imaginary accounts, cool old photos of places you ll recognize in Glasgow and amazing top facts and information, you will

discover things in Children s History of
Glasgow you never knew about your
town. Investigate the people and events
that have defined your home town:
Who was St Mungo? Where was James
Watt when he first thought of inventing
the steam engine?
**https://geni.us/historybookglasgow**

LOCHNESS

Printed in Great Britain
by Amazon

61692019R00117